SUNDAY BRUNCH
WITH THE WORLD MAKER

SUNDAY BRUNCH
WITH THE WORLD MAKER

Stefan Stenudd

Stefan Stenudd is a Swedish author, artist, and historian of ideas. He has published a number of books in Swedish as well as English, both fiction and non-fiction. Among the latter are books about Taoism, the cosmology of the Greek philosophers, the Japanese martial arts, Tarot, astrology, and an encyclopedia of life force concepts.

His novels explore existential subjects from stoneage drama to science fiction, but lately stay more and more focused on the present. He has written some plays for the stage and the screen. In the history of ideas he researches the thought patterns of creation myths, as well as Aristotle's *Poetics*. He is also an aikido instructor, 7 dan Aikikai, former Vice Chairman of the International Aikido Federation and Chairman of the Swedish Budo & Martial Arts Federation. He has his own extensive website:
 www.stenudd.com

Books by Stefan Stenudd:
Ever Young, 2017, 2018.
Sunday Brunch with the World Maker, 2016, 2018, 2020.
All's End, 2007, 2015.
Occasionally I Contemplate Murder, 2006, 2011, 2015.
Cosmos of the Ancients: The Greek Philosophers on Myth and Cosmology, 2007, 2011, 2015.
Tao Te Ching: The Taoism of Lao Tzu Explained, 2011, 2015.
Tao Quotes, 2013, 2015.
Tarot Unfolded: Imaginative Reading of the Divination Cards, 2012, 2015.
Life Energy Encyclopedia, 2009, 2015.
Qi: Increase Your Life Energy, 2008, 2009, 2015.
Aikido Principles, 2008, 2016.
Attacks in Aikido, 2008, 2009, 2015.
Aikibatto: Sword Exercises for Aikido Students, 2007, 2009.
Your Health in Your Horoscope: Introduction to Medical Astrology, 2009, 2015.

Sunday Brunch with the World Maker.
Copyright © Stefan Stenudd, 2016, 2018, 2020.
Book design by the author.
All rights reserved.
ISBN: 978-91-7894-085-1
Publisher: Arriba, Malmö, Sweden, info@arriba.se, www.arriba.se
Printed by Lightning Source.

And I cried for all the others
Till the day was nearly through,
For I realized that
God's a young man too.
>   *David Bowie, The Width of a Circle.*

The Long Way There

I walked right into it. Of course I did. From the moment I left my apartment in Malmö, Sweden, until I sat down at a table for two in the Peacock Alley of the Waldorf Astoria Hotel in Manhattan. Despite the spontaneity of my decisions leading me there, I could not have ended up anywhere else.

But I didn't know that yet.

*

Probably my path to this table, covered with an impeccable white cloth, started already in 1980. That year I spent a few months strolling the streets and avenues of Manhattan. It has been a vivid and cherished memory ever since.

I was 25 when I arrived on Good Friday, crossing the George Washington Bridge with a ridiculously big Chevy station wagon, which I soon had to abandon. It was from 1969, so it had done its duty.

Just hours after I crossed the bridge, it was closed to cars without additional passengers, due to a public transport strike. Everything is big in Manhattan. Commuting got very near chaos, when subways and buses stopped going.

The following Monday, the mayor of New York at the time, Edward Koch, greeted people who crossed the Brooklyn Bridge by foot to get to work, thanking them for their patience. Next morning he did it again, with a clerk holding an umbrella over his head, since it was raining. The third morning he didn't show up.

Soon, the public transport workers got what they wanted, and the strike was over. Like me more than three decades later, Mayor Koch didn't have much choice, whatever he may have imagined.

*

As soon as I had parked my Chevy and checked in to the Vanderbilt YMCA on 47th Street, I took the first of hundreds of strolls in Manhattan, immediately feeling right at home.

It was not only the ease of navigation, with each street and avenue numbered in a strict grid, making me find my way as easily as if I had been born there. Nor was it the vast number of strangers, all those unknowns faces never to be seen again, making me no more and no less of a stranger than anybody else.

I came to believe that the humongous quantity of people was what made me instantly belong. Back in 1980, that cigar shaped island had a million and a half inhabitants and almost as many commuted there every weekday. I believe it's about the same today. The sheer mass of humans had its gravitational pull. Once you were there you were a part of it, indistinguishable from the rest.

I loved it. Walking around in that melting pot of human existence, I was completely anonymous in a most tantalizing way. My personality did not deteriorate, but blended with everyone else. The gravity of our multitude made each of us a cell in one common body, lying at full length with its head on Inwood and its feet by Battery Park – or maybe the other way around.

The sensation reminded me of what the English rock artist Eric Burdon had sung, a mantra of the flower power 1960's, "We're all one."

I wanted to spend the rest of my life there, but I didn't

have much chance of affording it. Already the 13 dollars a day cost for my room at the Vanderbilt YMCA, a lodging relevant to the price, would be too much at length. I managed those few months with advances on the royalties for my Swedish astrology book, as of yet my only bestseller. But a bestseller in Sweden is quickly diluted in the publishing center of the world.

Still, living off a book when staying in Manhattan was spot on. While Los Angeles on the opposite side of the continent is mainly about movies, New York is the capital of literature. As a young writer, it was a heartwarming delight to visit the huge Dalton bookstore, a veritable temple of books. And the location – a skyscraper on 666 Fifth Avenue with the mythical street number in big red neon on top – could but make me smile mischievously. Literature should be that provocative.

So, I tried my best to find a way of remaining in Manhattan. I checked the possibilities for getting a green card to replace my tourist visa. A friend paired me up with a lawyer, who was an expert on making that happen. But he told me I would need to have something like 40,000 dollars on my bank account. I wasn't even able to come up with his fee.

*

I did have a literary agent for a while. That would solve it, if things had gone my way.

I had translated a science fiction story of mine, already published in Sweden, and sent it to Sanford J. Greenburger Associates, the agent of several prominent US writers – one of them being Kurt Vonnegut, whose books had inspired me to start my own writing. After just a few days, they called me to a meeting in their skyscraper midtown office, which happened to be just a few blocks away from the Vanderbilt YMCA.

It was the first time I was up in one of those things. An elevator so fast I felt the g-force took me halfway up a 40 floors building. That was quite enough for me. During the conversation with one of their agents, I had difficulties concentrating on our talk, since the view through the window behind her gave me vertigo.

Frankly, I was scared, holding on to my chair as if that would keep me any safer. My fantasy had a tendency to go wild in unfamiliar situations, imagining all kinds of mayhem, no matter how unlikely. I was embarrassed, thinking that my fear exposed me as a rural ignorant, who could not even handle something as commonplace in the big city as a skyscraper.

The agent didn't notice my trepidation, as far as I could tell. Or she was kind enough not to let me know. If she did, she might have interpreted it as an aspiring young writer's anxiety when coming so close to the big opportunity. It's hard to get an agent in New York. Well, everything is hard to get in New York.

Her name was Jill Stone, which sounded to me like the tough detective of a gruesome crime story – except for the fact that in 1980, there were no female action heroes in fiction. She loved my script, so I loved her. Also, the cheerful young woman was easy on the eyes.

She talked enthusiastically about the script, and about what she would do for it. My dream about staying in Manhattan quickly became plausible.

With a voice rising even more in excitement, she said that once the book got published in the USA, the agency had good connections to arrange for it to be published also in Japan! She pronounced the last word like a crescendo. I was confused. I thought US publication was the major thing, but

she shook her head. Then she repeated, as if mesmerized:
"Japan!"

We moved on to talk about my name. Americans could comfortably say Stefan, though their pronunciation differed quite a lot from what my mother called me. But my surname Stenudd, how would an American tongue manage its way around that?

Jill assured me it was a piece of cake. It was just how the English pronounced the word 'standard.' I could hear that it worked, somewhat, mainly by leaving the vowels out. But I had to hide my discomfort by the prospect of being named standard. That is far from flattering to any artist.

Anyway, the glorious prospect soon faded. Jill Stone bravely tried a few US publishers, who all rejected the script, and then she gave up.

I can't blame her. In hindsight, it was a script in dire need of editing. My treatment of the English language was clumsy, to put it mildly. An agent might forget about it, from pure enjoyment of the story, but a publisher needs to think about the work hours involved. It would take a bundle of them to get the script acceptable for publishing.

Nonetheless, I was proud to have had a US literary agent, albeit just for a while. And many years later I edited the script myself, as best I could, and got it published without the roundabout of having it solicited by an agent or approved by a publishing house. The Internet is a wonderful thing.

*

And I got to meet Kurt Vonnegut, back there in 1980. That's something. Not that the meeting was very fancy. A haphazard thing that could have been a paragraph in one of his books. Maybe just a sentence. Still, he seemed to know already in the beginning of his writing that anything seemingly haphazard really isn't. I was not to find it out until my next visit to Manhattan.

What led me to Vonnegut was the noise of Manhattan. It didn't subside until something like four o'clock in the morning, the hour of the wolf, and even then not for more than another hour. That was when I was able to go to sleep. Rarely sooner. If not clubbing, or playing the typewriter keys in my hotel room, I spent the noisy night hours strolling on town.

One such night, I was getting something to eat in a round-the-clock coffee shop a block or two from my Vanderbilt YMCA lodging. Making my order, I chatted joyously with the cute Puerto Rican girl behind the counter. One might even say I was flirting with her, in a casual way.

After a minute or two of this, I heard a heavy sigh from behind and turned around. I found myself looking right at somebody's chest. I had to tilt my head backwards to see the face. It was Kurt Vonnegut. I recognized him immediately, although I had only seen him on pictures and short TV interviews before.

At the coffee shop, he looked like the driver of the Phantom Chariot in the Swedish silent movie with that name from 1921. An image of sinister death. Tall, dark, dismal. That didn't stop me from starting a conversation with him. But Kurt Vonnegut was not amused. He must have regarded this lively youth as intentionally provocative to his own aging fatigue. He must have gotten the impression I was happy.

So, we didn't become buddies, but I did meet him. I had an agent for a moment. I talked face to face with my favorite writer for a moment. That was Manhattan. Everything was near, and yet so far away.

Still, I wanted more of it. Much more.

*

Returning to Sweden, I held on to my dream of settling in New York for good. What I did back in Sweden, I told myself, was just something to do in the meantime. But that meantime swelled into years and years.

Not until I had gotten a couple of years older than Kurt Vonnegut was when I met him, did I finally get around returning to Manhattan. But this time I had no intention of making it a one-way trip. I just couldn't see that happening. I went as a tourist to revisit that strange land, which had captured me long ago and remained a mirage in my mind.

I believed my trip to be on an impulse. I happened to have some money on my account – no 40,000 dollars, but enough for a comfortable week-long stay. I traveled coach, of course, and chose a reasonably priced hotel. Thereby, a Sunday brunch at Waldorf Astoria was well within my means.

I had done it with a New York friend back in 1980. It is a mystery how I could afford it. We probably had some budget version of the brunch, or it was significantly cheaper back then.

Anyway, although my memory of that brunch remained through the years, it had no prominent place in my recollection of Manhattan. It was more of a sightseeing thing, and those have never been the top of my list. The majestic extravagance of the place did make an impression on me, but not tremendously so since I had already explored a number of authentic European palaces. If you've seen one...

The reason I wanted to have another Sunday brunch at the famous hotel was to compare my impressions after the experience of twelve years as the restaurant critic of a newspaper in my hometown.

I call it restaurant critic, not food critic, since the job is about so much more than the food, if properly done. One should consider the ambiance, the service, the wine list, the background music, other guests frequenting the establishment, and so on. The whole experience. I even reviewed the restrooms.

I had quit that job before deciding on the trip to Manhattan, but after twelve years I still had the urge to test restaurants wherever I went. I was not fed up with it, although I had enough of writing newspaper columns about it.

And it was my quitting that job giving me the funds needed.

I got a full year's wage when leaving, as a sort of bonus for the long time of service. Although it was more money than I'd ever had on my bank account before, it was far from enough to migrate to Manhattan. But it was more than enough to go there for a week to reminisce and rediscover. Adding some culinary expeditions seemed appropriate.

As a critic, I had my share of fine dining, so that didn't tempt me much. Actually, I had come to almost loathe it.

When done expertly and artistically, a culinary multi-course dinner can be a sublime sensual experience, something that lingers on in the memory of one's palate for the rest of one's life. Then the price tag, no matter how steep, is negligible.

But if there are even the minutest flaws in the dishes or in the composition they create from the little *amuse-bouche* served to hint a theme, until the pieces of candy accompanying the bill at the end – then it all becomes a tedious display of presumption. That happens more often than not.

In such cases, reading the bill is an agonizing end note to the concert. I even get guilt feelings from spending so much money on something so ridiculously extravagant.

Of course, that was easier to get over during my years

as a restaurant critic, when the newspaper covered my bill.

Even in those days, though, I was irritated by the fine dining basic recipe of adding expensive ingredients, as if that would automatically make the dish delicious, no matter how they were cooked or combined. Lobster, caviar, goose liver and truffle can certainly be delicious, but not when mainly used to defend the steep price of a meal.

A lot of ingredients regarded as plain can create equal sensations – for example, just about every vegetable if chosen and treated with proper care.

But the thing with the Waldorf Astoria Sunday brunch is something else than the food, although there is plenty of it. It is the fancy setting and the long history. This Sunday brunch is an archetype all of its own.

That made me decide to give it another go, decades later – in spite of the ridiculously steep price even for two meals combined into one: 120 dollars plus tax and the mandatory tip called by its gilded name gratuity.

*

When I booked the brunch, I could do it in my own name, which was a thrilling sensation. Working as a restaurant critic, I had been as secretive as a spy during the cold war. Even on my newspaper, only a few persons knew who their restaurant critic was. There was a lot of hush-hush involved in the routines.

I didn't have a desk at the newspaper. I never visited the place. Instead, I worked freelance, and any of the rare meetings with one of the few staff members knowing me took place elsewhere. If I needed to call them on the phone, I used an alias we had agreed on. I sent my texts directly to the editor-in-chief and my bills to the newspaper's CFO.

I didn't even tell my friends.

There is certain arithmetic to secrets. A friend will only tell one or two others, but they in turn will tell more people, who will spread it with no care at all. The longer from the source, the less discretion. Secrecy simply demands silence.

All that secrecy was the most straining part of the job. Having a substantial part of my life concealed, as if non-existent, kept me constantly on guard. It was necessary and I quickly adapted to it, but it was nevertheless a burden. Getting that burden off my chest would take quite some time. I might still be working on it.

Well, I digress.

This Is Not Right

After more than 35 years I finally returned to Manhattan, immediately exalted by a strange mixture of memories and fresh impressions. The turmoil, the intensity, the buildings penetrating the sky and concealing it, the streets and avenues where countless cars impatiently competed to move at all, the wide sidewalks packed with people strangely often walking in unison as if marching, the noise from multiple sources blending into a buzz that became a kind of silence.

It was good to be back.

In no time, I was out walking the streets just like I had done in 1980, getting just as invigorated by it.

Walking is what you do in Manhattan. That's the main treat the island has to offer. It was also what I was set on doing, already when I planned the trip. Like back in the day. Walk and walk and walk. Already on the day of my arrival, I wandered for miles without feeling any fatigue. Manhattan had not changed at all. I doubt that it can.

The following Sunday morning at my hotel, I had a minimal breakfast of coffee, orange juice and a slice of toast – really just to wake up. I was booked to have my Waldorf Astoria brunch at eleven. That would give me a few hours to indulge in the buffet. I dressed up as much as I felt compelled to do, which was my plain black suit and a rather colorful shirt. Just to make sure, I rolled up a tie and put it in a pocket.

I often use a patterned shirt to sort of conceal the fact that I don't wear a tie. Not that I hate ties. Actually, I find them quite decorative if chosen with taste. But they are not that very comfortable and they tend to make me feel like I'm stuck in a garrote. Furthermore, I'm no master at tying them, always needing several tries before I get the front end sufficiently long.

Another good thing about patterned shirts, by the way, is that they don't need to be ironed very meticulously.

I chose shoes for comfort rather than style, since I decided to walk to the Waldorf Astoria. I hoped the hotel staff would refrain from inspecting me that far down.

The walk to the Waldorf Astoria building, though, was too short to get me into much of the vagabond mood I aimed for. It didn't even stir my appetite. But that didn't worry me. When I was a restaurant critic it often happened that I had to stuff an already full belly. I could manage that.

*

The front of the hotel was just as splendid as I remembered it. Art Deco gone wild. A lot of gold, of course, also in the sign high above the entrance. Its classic font read, with capital letters, THE WALDORF-ASTORIA.

I paused a little while in front of it, amused by the presumptuous THE, as if there can be only one. Nowadays, there are more Waldorf Astoria hotels around the world. Still, in this case it was not completely uncalled for. The lack of the word hotel was also easy to explain. In spite of the many luxury rooms, this is an archetype that just happens to be a hotel, too.

The building itself, though, impressed me much less, except for its size. Just a flat gray surface with too many similar rectangles.

I eagerly entered the foyer, knowing full well that it would dazzle me. It had done so at my previous visit. I remembered that it had felt just like a royal palace.

To my surprise, I was not as flabbergasted as I had expected to be. It was big, certainly, and lavishly decorated in Art Deco style. Lots of marble in light colors and many gilded details. It reeked of luxury.

But it was not a palace, in my mind. Just something aspiring to be one. It lacked age, the most majestic thing there is. I had a faint impression of standing in a Potemkin village.

Blatant luxury in itself tends to make me uncomfortable, almost nauseated. I can enjoy the splendor if it is done in taste. If not, I am just reminded of how unfair this world is. Some get it all. That's nothing to brag about. Flaunting it is nothing but vulgar.

This foyer lacked the grace and refinement to excuse its shameless display of absurd wealth.

Had they renovated the interior of the hotel since my visit in 1980? That is something easily going bad. Or had I become much more accustomed to majestic architecture than I was in my twenties? Whatever the case, I found myself puzzled by not being baffled.

As I continued to the main lobby, I started to wonder if the forthcoming bill would give me an aftertaste of guilt.

The main lobby was different from the foyer, somewhat toned down. Its colors were darker, with dimmed light and a lot of brown on the walls. The floor was covered by a carpet with a multitude of decorative patterns, where light blue was the basic background color. The center piece was a big clock, some ten feet tall in all. It was covered by bronze reliefs and crowned with a gilded statue of liberty. Quite too much.

Strangely, I could not recall anything of this scenery from 1980. Not even the clock – but that was something I would not have given more than a glance in any case. I have never been attracted by functional objects being so elaborate that their function gets camouflaged. Less is more.

In addition, this was the time of Sunday brunch, so the clock was surrounded by buffet tables. They spread over most of the lobby area, heavily packed with food of all kinds. This would take some time to explore, no doubt. The only thing separating the buffet area from the regular lobby traffic was a line of red ropes attached to brass poles.

I did appreciate the courage of integrating the brunch with the lobby, where hotel guests were constantly checking in and out. It might not be very hygienic, but it made the whole area a lively melting pot.

One could not get bored in this scenery. Also, the vast display of food made the clock all but disappear, from which it benefited.

The lobby had room for a grand piano, which was played rather softly, even subdued, by a middle-aged man who was also singing into a microphone. I presumed that this was mainly intended for the restaurant guests, but any visitor to the lobby would be able to hear it just as well.

As I passed him, he was performing some pop song that might have been a hit a while back, but I would not be able to sing along. His voice was of the kind that is as gentle as it is forgettable.

Not every pianist is candy to the ears, but no doubt it adds so much more to the ambiance than recorded music through loudspeakers. This one neither irritated nor appealed to me significantly, which was perfect. He would not distract me from my meal. He knew that he was not the main attraction here.

*

Also the dining area of the Peacock Alley was in immediate connection to the lobby. Even the carpet was the same. I recognized nothing of the scenery from my previous visit. Had it not been as memorable as I surmised?

A hostess was ready to take me to my table. She was in her twenties, slim and elegant with moderate makeup and a black business dress. She knew how to be pleasantly polite without overdoing it. I got the impression that she was not working there just to bide her time before a Broadway career.

On the way to my table, I asked the hostess if the lobby had been changed in some way since 1980. She told me that there had been a ten-year renovation started in the mid-1980's by a famous architect, returning the hotel to its original grandeur, as it were. It cost 150 million.

"That's a lot of Sunday brunches," I said, just to avoid making a derogatory comment.

She smiled politely as she led me on to a far corner, aiming at the tables next to a kitchen entrance. That's not what I would call a good start. I glanced around at the many empty tables with prettier settings and closer to the buffet. Should I bring the subject up or not? New York is not the most famous for its patience and benevolence.

The hostess stopped so suddenly that I almost bumped in to her.

"No, this is not right," she mumbled to herself, sounding very confused.

Then she turned around and had us go back to the center of the dining area. She showed me to a table for two, right next to one of the many big black marble pillars. It was as close to the buffet area as would be comfortable. Quite ideal. So, I was not going to ask what made her change her mind about my seating. Don't look a gift horse in the mouth.

When I worked as a restaurant critic, something like

this would make me suspicious. Were they on to my identity and was I getting VIP treatment because of it? But in no way did the hostess show that the change of seating had anything to do with me. She probably got it wrong to begin with, and realized it along the way. An honest mistake.

Anyway, I was happy with the outcome. Looking around, I got the impression that this must be one of the very best tables, at least of the small ones. It had a good view of most of the place, with the pillar on one side adding some privacy. And it was at a comfortable distance from the pianist, so his playing would not swarm my ears. Perfect. I ceased to worry about feeling anguish when it would be time for the bill.

She pulled out the chair for me and gave some brief instructions, pointing at the buffet area. Then she introduced my waiter, who had appeared discreetly at that moment. It was a man close to my age, with a tired look partly camouflaged by a scant smile.

With quite another kind of smile, showing just about all of her shiny white teeth, the hostess wished me a very pleasant meal. Then she was off.

I told my waiter that I intended to start with a glass of Champagne from the bar I had already spotted when entering. So, he was off as well.

I leaned back in my chair, giving myself a moment to take everything in before getting started with the brunch.

The chair was another thing I used to consider in my restaurant reviews. This one was kind of comfortable, and it had room for a person of a volume surpassing mine, but its horizontally curved backrest forced my body into sort of a crouching position. Especially when having a multi-course meal, this is not ideal.

I reminded myself that at least the seating location was great.

*

I got up from my seat to have a brief tour of the buffet, which was divided into a dozen sections with at least an equal amount of themes. After mere glimpses of the abundance it had to offer, I went to the bar to order a glass of Champagne.

There was already a formation of flute glasses semi-filled with the bubbly elixir. That's practically sacrilege with a beverage excelling at the instant of its pouring. I wanted a freshly poured glass. I also had questions for the bartender about the type of Champagne served. I was doing my thing.

I explained how I preferred my Champagne. They got the glass right. Coupes are just for stapling, not for drinking, since they don't show the bubbles other than on the surface. In a flute, you can see them form a tiny pillar in the center. Champagne bubbles should be small and orderly, in a multitude that lasts very long – if you let them. But good Champagne you can't resist drinking quickly, in big gulps.

That's the most important characteristic. In spite of the price, you should find yourself emptying a bottle without realizing it until you hold the bottle upside down and the last drops make their kamikaze into the glass. That is why a single glass is next to meaningless. There really has to be a bottle, or the experience is over before it has begun.

As for the taste, I genuinely dislike the fashion of wanting a pungent scent of bread. Why spend money on liquid baguette? It should be vibrantly fresh, like children playing in a park, and needs no complication to justify its existence. Oddly, the most enjoyable Champagnes are not the most expensive ones.

The bartender assured me that I would be pleased with the Champagne he had to offer, and I brought a freshly poured glass back to my table. Sitting there, taking big gulps of the bubbly, I glanced at the empty chair on the other side of the table.

It wouldn't be empty for long.

Enter the Dragon

Just as I grabbed the armrests of my chair to get up and have a first go at the buffet, a young man appeared by the table and asked me with an extremely mellow voice, sounding like the vinyl recording of a jazz singer played on a tube amp hi-fi:

"Excuse me, sir. Would you mind terribly if I took this seat?"

He pointed to the vacant chair on the other side of my table. I looked at it, and then I looked around in the Peacock Alley. There were several empty tables.

"The hostess told me that the small ones are booked," he explained, not bothering to look where I did. "And they really don't want me to block any of the bigger tables, as you surely understand."

I nodded, although I was not thrilled by the idea of sharing this experience with a stranger. Then I took a closer look at him.

He was a very handsome young man, hardly any older than twenty. Rich black hair, distinguished features, marked eyebrows and lips, sort of Japanese eyes, slender and kind of fragile. He looked like the movie actor Ezra Miller in his adolescence.

"I get that a lot," he said with a faint smile.

"Get what?"

"I'm an Ezra Miller look-alike. I don't know how many times I've heard it. So, when I saw the surprise in your eyes I thought you were thinking the same."

"I was. And you are. Does it bother you?"

"Not the slightest."

I thought that couldn't be true. Or he had found out it got him laid. Suddenly his smile widened. I was again confused.

"So?" he inquired.

"Oh, I'm sorry. Please sit down."

I gestured to the seat. Although I usually prefer solitude at restaurants, especially good ones, I looked forward to have this beautiful face in front of me. It would be yet another delicatessen – or solace, if the food proved to be less than formidable.

*

Beauty is the foremost, maybe only, evidence of anything divine in this universe. We all worship it, whatever we pretend. And this young man was certainly good enough for an altar.

His eyes were just as dark brown as mine had been in my youth, I don't remember how long ago. Their darkness gave them a deep sense of melancholia. Staring into them for long would probably bring tears to my eyes. But his lips were smiling. It was an anomaly that intrigued me.

It reminded me of Kurt Vonnegut, in some odd way. The very entertaining writer had been as grim as the driver of the Phantom Chariot, taking the dead to their final destination. Humor seems to evoke misery, its absolute counterpart. Or the other way around.

The young man wore a brilliantly white shirt and a black suit, which looked like it must be Armani. It was a perfect fit and he had the slender body to carry it. No tie. That would be overdoing it.

Still, the shirt was buttoned all the way up. It was the right thing to do with this outfit, though not the sexiest option. That impeccable white shirt open to the chest would surely be attractive on such a beauty, but also quite vulgar.

Once seated, he extended his hand to me.

"I'm Cael. Pleased to meet you."

"Me too," I said, grabbing his hand. "I'm Stefan."

I was glad he presented himself only with his first name, as I do. That makes even a brief encounter much less formal, less of an inspection.

His hand was warm and so dry, there was friction when I shook it. This gave a slightly tickling sensation that I could feel right through my body. I almost forgot to let go of his hand.

"I see you emptied your glass," he said after getting his hand back. "It must have been good, then. May I bring you a refill as I get one for myself?"

"It was alright," I replied.

"Good enough for the whole brunch?"

"I was planning on it, although that might mean I need to skip some dishes of the buffet."

"Then I'll try to get us a bottle," he said as he stood up.

"I'm not sure they allow that," I commented, but he was already on his way.

I looked at him go. He had a smooth stride, almost as if he was sailing on the thick light blue carpet with diamond patterns, although his shiny black shoes were formal with hard soles.

When he disappeared behind a pillar, I looked around in the dining room. We were far from alone, but there were plenty of empty chairs all over. That Cael could hardly have had any trouble getting a table of his own. Why did he want to sit at mine?

I remembered the multitude of human desperation I had witnessed back in 1980. At that time, New York was a jungle where only the fittest survived. In one way or other, everyone was a hustler, given the chance. I doubted that this had changed.

Maybe Cael was targeting me for some cash, whatever he was prepared to offer for it. He might even have told the waiter that I was paying for both of us.

I made a note in my mind to somehow check that out discreetly.

*

Then he was back, with a Champagne bottle in one hand and two flute glasses in the other. It was a Laurent-Perrier, a wine house with which I have had several pleasant experiences.

"You could do that?" I asked with some surprise. In my experience, few restaurants were inclined to bend the rules for their patrons.

"It was no problem at all," he replied as he put the glasses on the table. "I simply bought it."

"Oh, what do I owe you?"

He just waved his free hand in response. Then he gallantly filled our glasses to the rim and sat down. He raised his glass.

"Cheers!" he said, moving the glass towards me.

"Cheers!" I repeated with slightly less enthusiasm, bringing my glass to kiss his.

The clink was rather muffled, because the glasses were full. We hurried to do something about it. But he was quick to refill them, although they were not yet empty.

The Champagne was *demi-sec*, which surprised me until I remembered American fondness for the basic tastes, the ones already the tongue distinguishes. But it was not too sweet, so I could actually enjoy it.

"What do you say, should we explore the buffet?"

I asked him, mainly to avoid drinking with the indicated speed. "Are you hungry?"

"Always," he said with a grin. "You be my guide."

"But I've just been here once before, and that was ages ago."

"Come on now, Stefan," he protested, pronouncing my name in a perfectly Swedish fashion.

I was amazed, but had no time to comment on it.

"I get the feeling you're familiar with these kinds of things," he continued and stood up. "How do you plan to approach the abundance we're up against?"

We started towards the big area of buffet tables, where several cooks in the traditional white apparel, *toque blanche* high hat and all, were busy attending to all the dishes on display. They had their sleeves rolled up, which was more practical than stylish. The left chests of the uniforms were decorated with the monogram WA.

"Well, I usually take a good look around, before I tackle a buffet. I don't want to try it all, but search for the jewels, the things that tempt me the very most."

"I can relate to that," Cael intervened, nodding a few times.

"Then there's the order of things. I don't know how Americans do it, but I'm Swedish, so I like to handle any buffet as I would the smorgasbord." I made an effort to pronounce the Swedish term in an English way. I could feel that it made my lips move awkwardly.

"And how is that?"

"It's quite simple, maybe even universal. We start with fish, then the meat."

"I knew that."

"There is a lot of fish on the Swedish smorgasbord buffet. Pickled herring in particular. I don't think we'll find that here. We pickle raw herring in many different ways, and that's what we start with. Often, I get no further than that, if they know their herring. If I'm not full by then, it's time for the salmon. And after that the boiled stockfish with béchamel sauce, seasoned with crushed allspice. I love that, when they cook it tenderly. But usually, it's only served at Christmas time."

"I can hear you're building an appetite. But I guess we'll find none of that, except salmon. Would they have salmon good enough to satisfy a Scandinavian?"

"Well, they probably get it from Norway. The question is what they do with it."

"Let's check that out right now," Cael said, hurrying his steps. "I knew you'd be the perfect tour guide."

"Salmon would be great with the Champagne. As would practically any seafood, of course."

*

We quickly found the table with a veritable erupting volcano of seafood, and filled the plates we picked from a pile nearby. The plates were plain white, without any other decoration than their waved rims.

As expected, there was no herring, but Maine lobster tails and claws, Canadian snow crab, oysters and peeled jumbo shrimps in abundance. Salmon, too, which was smoked with several different flavorings and cut in thin slices. Its distinct orange-red color was a giveaway that it was farmed – but in the Catskills, and not Norway.

I frowned at my own ignorance. Of course they knew how to farm salmon in the USA, too.

"I tend to prefer wild salmon to the farmed one," I told Cael as we picked our slices from the plate. "It's not at all as colorful, but its taste is more refined, although vague. Unfortunately, it's hard to find nowadays."

"That's how it goes," he commented as he added another slice to his plate. "I'll weep when I eat it."

"We'll find solace in the Champagne."

We returned to our table, finding that the waiter had brought an ice bucket on its own stand for the Champagne. I refilled our glasses and we started to dig in, staying silent for the first few bites.

I would have begun with the oysters, but Cael gave me no chance. He was most eager to try the salmon and I followed his lead. Then we gulped another glass of Champagne.

"So, how about it?" Cael asked, looking right at me with some anticipation. "How did you find the salmon?"

"Like usual abroad. The texture is a bit too rubbery, almost like chewing gum. It should practically melt in your mouth. You should hardly need your teeth to eat it."

"With this one I certainly do. Not that I mind, but someday I have to try the Scandinavian version of it."

"Oh, they have a lot of it in Canada, too."

I took another bite. I was not too thrilled by the distinct flavors they had added to the salmon in the smoking. Bourbon, pepper and what-not. That hid its own subtle taste. And maybe the excessive smoking of it was responsible for the texture. I didn't mention it to Cael, since he seemed quite happy with the salmon.

"In the early twentieth century," I continued, "there was a law in Sweden stating that workers should not be served salmon more than a certain number of days a week. The fish was so commonplace back then, people risked malnutrition from eating just about only salmon. Nowadays, it's more of a luxury."

"Also in Sweden?"

I nodded as I turned my attention to the oysters.

"We still eat it a lot, but it's far from cheap."

"What can you do?" Cael said with a playful kind of sigh. "Money makes the world go around."

"That's precisely the rancid aftertaste of any gourmet meal."

He looked up from his plate, where he was still at the salmon, and made sure to catch my eyes before speaking.

"Would that be something akin to the little death of which the French speak?"

*

Both the subject and his elaborate way of formulating the question made the erotic implication evident. So did his eyes fixed on mine and the vague tendency of a smile on his lips. I could feel my cheeks blushing and hoped it went unnoticed. Was he flirting with old me?

"Well," I replied, trying a smile, "there's also the old saying, credited to Galen: 'After intercourse, every animal is sad – except woman and the rooster.'"

He laughed. It was neither loud nor long, but melodic, like a xylophone solo. It was heartwarming.

"Isn't that a good cue to start with the oysters," he said as he did so.

Oysters, the aphrodisiac of Casanova. Now I was sure he was flirting, or at least playing with the idea.

I felt flattered, not only considering our age difference. I could almost be his grandfather. The days were long gone when I managed to imagine having the looks with a magnetic influence on others.

It also made me even more wary.

"As for woman," I resumed after trying an oyster, "the ancient idea was probably that she was the one gaining something, whereas the man lost that same something, being the seed of reproduction. I think they believed that the embryo was in that seed alone. They knew nothing about any X and Y chromosomes. And Galen had all kinds of ideas about the different bodily fluids, as did most ancient cultures. Spilling the seed would be regarded as losing some of one's vitality."

"And the rooster?"

"Who knows?" I replied, getting relieved by feeling that my cheeks were returning to their normal temperature. "In past times, everybody had seen roosters copulate. Maybe they hurry tirelessly from one hen to the next."

I remembered a humorous song that was a big hit in Sweden back in the 1960's, performed by a famous folk singer. It told the story of a rooster picking feathers from a particularly pretty hen instead of mounting her. When this had gone on for a while, the hen was fed up and asked why. "Oh, I'll mount you," the rooster assured her, "but I want you naked when I do."

Cael suddenly burst into laughter. It almost made me drop the oyster I had just picked up.

"It was just something that crossed my mind," he explained when the laughter had died out, which didn't take long. As he saw that I was still confused, he added, "I won't bore you with it. I'm sure you know it already."

He placed the empty oyster shell on the plate and grabbed the next one.

"So, what do you think about the oysters?" he asked.

"Fresh," I replied. "That's about it with them. But a bit too big for my taste. I prefer the small ones that the French also favor. Less is more, you know."

Cael lifted the oyster and held it in front of his Japanese eyes. It made him slightly cross-eyed.

"Big is the American way," he said. Then he shoved the oyster into his mouth and swallowed it. "What do you say, we try the caviar?"

He refilled our glasses, again to the rim. I looked at my plate, where a lobster tail and a few peeled jumbo shrimps remained. Cael's plate looked just about the same.

"Maybe we should really have started with the caviar," I said. "But this is good company for it." I pointed to my plate.

"Still, shouldn't we get fresh plates?" Cael inquired, sounding rather excited. "After all, it is caviar."

I had to agree.

"I'm curious about how they solved this," I mumbled as I prepared to stand up. "I seriously doubt that we'll be able to scoop up a lot of Russian or Iranian caviar. That would go way beyond even the steep price of this brunch."

"Have you done a lot of caviar scooping, by any chance?"

I shook my head. Cael was not standing up yet, so I leaned back on my chair.

"I've never filled my belly with it. The closest I got to such gluttony was in Prague in the early 1990's, soon after they were liberated from the Soviet dominance. They sold a lot of Russian caviar on the streets. The prices were ridiculously low, so I got some. But that ended in a year or two."

"It was nice while it lasted, I bet."

"It was. Oddly, though, I still have one of those cans in my fridge back home. Maybe it's not the same when you get it that cheap."

"Or maybe you're not that fond of it."

"Well, I can live without it. It's quite salty. On the other hand, it's probably the most delicious salt in the world. Just as the legendary sweet wine Chateau d'Yquem is the most delicious sugar."

"Stefan, it sounds to me like you've had your share of gluttony."

Again I marveled at his exact Swedish pronunciation

of my name. I looked at his amused face for a few seconds before replying.

"Sort of. Back home, I was a restaurant critic for twelve years."

"I knew it!" Cael exclaimed with a grin.

*

Telling people about that part of my past was sort of therapy, after so many years of needing to keep it a secret. Even long after I quit the job, I felt relief every time I mentioned it to somebody, especially and usually on a restaurant. Maybe I did it too often.

With Cael, I had at least waited until it felt kind of silly to hide it any longer.

"It was not so much gluttony as it was a job," I explained.

"But what a job!" he insisted.

"On good restaurants, surely. But imagine having to force down a seven course meal when already the amuse-bouche at the start is close to disgusting. Also, I insisted on reviewing restaurants all over the scale, from cheap joints around the corner to gourmet extravaganzas. I even reviewed McDonald's."

"And how was it?"

"Bland," I said.

Cael let out a few xylophone tones of laughter.

I checked around briefly to see if anyone had heard. That was a reflex from the time when I had to stay in hiding. But no one was near enough to hear us.

It made Cael laugh anew.

"Okay," he said when the laughter had died out, "I get that it was a job. But don't try to tell me that it was drab."

"It was, when the restaurant was. Quite a lot of them

were, to be honest. I had to struggle with myself to come up with a three thousand characters text."

"They had to be that long?"

"Not exactly. But I couldn't stop myself from trying to get as near to that number as possible, every time. I'm kind of manic that way."

"A perfectionist."

"I guess so. Even if it kills me."

"Well, so far it hasn't."

I shrugged my shoulders.

"Sometimes after stuffing myself with a multi-course meal, it felt like I was getting quite close."

"Couldn't you eat parts of the servings, just enough to get the taste?"

"That would immediately make the waiters suspicious. I didn't have to eat it all, but most of it. Well, almost all. Otherwise they'd start speculating."

"That's right. You had to be incognito."

"Yes, I was a veritable secret agent. I had to be very cautious. Some restaurants were really on guard, just about all the time. We used all kinds of precautions, and still my editor-in-chief thought I would be revealed in a year and a half. I managed for twelve. A few suspected me, but none were certain, as far as I know."

The smile playing on Cael's lips showed how amused he was about those past ordeals of mine. I had no trouble understanding him. Me too, I found it amusing – in hindsight.

When living it, I found it quite nerve-racking at times.

"How did you ever manage?"

"For the first few years, I had a foolproof strategy of playing a fool. A silly guest, seemingly ignorant of anything culinary. I asked stupid questions, showed a delighted smile at just about anything, and so on. They couldn't imagine that the grim critic, whose reviews reeked of authority, could be this buffoon."

I made a silly face with a ridiculously wide grin to illustrate my point. Again, Cael let out a little xylophone solo.

"You must have been a good actor. I wonder if I would have fallen for it."

His penetrating eyes suggested that he would not. It struck me that there probably was a lot more going on behind his forehead than his words suggested.

Again, the thought crossed my mind that Cael might be some kind of con-man. He had that devastating charm making a victim totally enjoy the experience, whatever the cost of it. I decided to stay on guard, although at the same time wondering if I would manage. Maybe I was already seduced, unable to defend myself against what might come.

"At length, that had to change," I said, continuing our conversation in an effort to hide my wariness. "Gradually, as they started to recognize my face, I shifted to what signified most of their patrons – someone enjoying a good meal and getting it frequently. When they acknowledged that they'd seen me before, I gladly admitted to it, and I could even have some chit-chat with them. If I didn't, they would surely compute. Also, the restaurants that were important enough to be reviewed regularly, I visited many times without writing about it. For twelve years I rarely had other meals at home than breakfast."

"You poor thing," Cael said teasingly.

"Nowadays, I do a lot of home cooking. To me, it has an exotic flare. Nothing fancy, mind you. Just simple things that are quick to cook."

"I find that hard to believe."

"Believe it. In the beginning, I got the habit of making my meals in the time it took to boil the potatoes. That would be twenty to twenty-five minutes, but since I cut them up in pieces it was done in ten. Now, I've let go of that, but it still rarely takes more than half an hour."

"Instant cooking."

"Indeed. I guess that would bring it close to Japanese and Italian cuisine, in a way. But I make ordinary things like roast chicken legs, oven baked cod, and pan-fried rib eye steak with a vinaigrette salad. What I enjoy the most is just about anything oven baked. The oven is a master at enriching the flavors and making the texture of the food perfect."

"How about salmon?"

"Sure. But it's hard to find a really good one in Swedish grocery stores." Noticing Cael's surprise, I added, "It's crazy, I know. But salmon has become an industry. It's a fish that's at its best served raw, not cooked, but then it has to be of fine quality. And fresh! The best salmon I've had was in Japan, although I believe they get it all the way from Norway. The Japanese sure know how to treat fish. In Sweden, it's kind of a lottery."

"So, how does it compare to the salmon here at the Waldorf?"

"This one is smoked, which tends to dry it and make it more rubbery. I prefer marinating it in the way we call gravlax in Sweden. Then it keeps its tenderness. Or plain salted."

"You mean we aren't off to a good start?"

"There's a lot yet to be tested," I replied, waving a hand in the direction of the buffet. "We should find plenty to tickle our taste buds. But I have to say, in my experience quantity is never an adequate substitute for quality."

"You are a hard one to please, aren't you?"

"Since I started home cooking regularly, I've found that it makes me even more picky than I was as a restaurant critic. Extremely few restaurant meals leave me satisfied. Or maybe it just bothers me that now I have to pay for them myself, instead of getting paid to have them."

"That would worsen the aftertaste significantly," Cael commented with a wide smile. "I'm curious about your judgment, when we reach the end of this buffet."

The Arts

We paused to have another sip of the Champagne. I tried to observe Cael closely and yet with some discretion. I probably wasn't very good at it, but he was kind enough to look away, as if having a moment of daydreaming.

I marveled again at how handsome he was, the young Ezra Miller lookalike. It was those Japanese eyes on an otherwise Caucasian face, quite pale at that, making his features transcend. And the black hair in careless tangles. Those who are really beautiful don't bother to enhance it.

For some reason, I was particularly confused by the fact that he had the features of an adolescent Ezra Miller, instead of what the actor looked like presently. As if that made it even less probable. I knew I was silly, but the sensation was there anyway. It made him kind of unreal, like the figure of a dream.

Male beauty is at its peak in adolescence. This has been known in the arts since ancient times. Before that age men lack grandeur, and after it their features harden.

With women, it is quite different, although today's aesthetic ideals don't recognize it. They celebrate the looks of women in their youth, discarding them as soon as they show signs of aging. Still, a lot of women famous for their ravishing beauty are older than that, before making us gasp when seeing them on the movie screen or the stage. As Eartha Kitt sang, "Life made me beautiful at forty."

It could be a balance thing, like yin and yang. Young men have a female streak and women approaching their middle-age get a touch of something male about them. There has to be some yang in the yin and yin in the yang, as the dots show in the ancient symbol of that duality.

There was definitely a feminine streak in Cael's appearance. His slenderness, his elegance, his smooth skin and delicate facial features. He would probably be sensational in drag. As I thought so, I could feel myself starting to blush again.

"How about you, then, Cael," I inquired, mainly to snap out of my speculations and my blatant staring. "You must be a passionate gourmet to spend so much money on a brunch."

He returned his dark Japanese eyes to me. They were easy to drown in.

"Not really. I'm just what they call independently wealthy." He added with a wink, "I hope that doesn't make you think less of me."

Just that wink made me blush anew, though briefly.

"Not at all," I assured him, although that wasn't completely true. "Have you come into an inheritance, if I may ask?"

He chuckled, mainly to himself, while his fingers played ever so lightly on the Champagne glass resting momentarily on the table.

"Not at all," he assured me. "I made all the money myself." He seemed to find his words rather amusing. His amusement increased as he added, "It's not difficult at all, once you know how."

Not for him, I thought, keeping it to myself. With his good looks there would be several ways to earn a lot of cash. I decided not to pursue the issue any further. For some reason, he broke out into yet another xylophone laughter.

"So, how about some caviar now?" he asked and stood up as soon as his laughter had ended, which did not take long. "The topic of our conversation kind of demands it."

It was my time to laugh, although little more than a chuckle.

*

We grabbed new plates by the buffet and found our way to the caviar. There were four different kinds in glass bowls of decent sizes – paddlefish, golden whitefish, Tobiko flying fish, and trout. No Russian or Iranian. That would ruin even the mighty Waldorf Astoria.

I took a spoonful of each, but then an extra spoon of the trout roe. Its brilliant orange color was irresistible, glimmering like jewels. It must be rainbow trout, I concluded. Those shiny marbles were smaller than salmon roe, but not by much.

The caviar bowls were a bit elevated from the table, on their own shelf, as they should be. Square shaped white bowls below contained the conventional accoutrements, such as crème fraîche, chopped shallots, chives and red onion.

There were also mini-sized blinis that looked quite cute. With caviar, I prefer simple toast, but the little blinis would do as a substitute.

I also added quite generously with crème fraîche, chopped red onion, and – after some hesitation – chives to the plate. Cael was watching and copying me.

"Have you tried caviar before?" I asked him as we were filling our plates.

"Russian more than the other stuff," he replied. "Trout seems to be your favorite."

"That, or salmon, and cisco. There's a fine cisco roe from Kalix, way up north in Sweden. Maybe salmon tops it all, at length. It's a sensation for several of the senses."

"That could be a marketing slogan."

We headed back to our table.

"The Japanese are very fond of herring roe," I resumed as we walked our way in zigzag around tables and pillars. "There, it's very exclusive. They have it at New Year, I've heard. In Sweden it's by far the most common fish since ages, and quite cheap. But we don't eat the roe, for some reason."

"Have you tried it?"

"In Japan, yes. On nigiri sushi. I think it's the texture they like so much. The taste is rather bland, but it's crunchy. That's fun for the teeth and works very well as a contrast to the superbly soft sushi rice."

"I have to try it sometime."

"It's not common. A Japanese friend of mine brought me to a splendid sushi place by the Little Fish Market in Tokyo. They had it, although it was in the early fall. I can't remember seeing it in other sushi bars, but I'm not sure."

*

We reached our table. The plates we had left behind, with some lobster and shrimp, had been removed. The waiter must have thought that we were finished with them.

"Just as well," I said. "I'm not so fond of lobster served cold. That hides a lot of its taste and makes the meat a bit tough, kind of like chewing a knitted glove. I think it's best grilled."

"How about the shrimps? They were cold, too."

"That works. We may have to refill on those. Also, both would be kind of nice to try with the caviar."

"There's still time," Cael said as he filled our glasses.

I had decided it was my turn, but he beat me to it.

I looked at my plate, where each caviar had its own neat pile. Then I had a small sample of the paddlefish caviar on the tip of my knife. That was the one I was the most curious about, never having tried it before.

"I get the impression you've been to Japan a lot," Cael said, looking at me trying the paddlefish caviar, instead of exploring what was on his own plate.

"Not really. Just five times or so, always because of aikido."

"Ah," Cael said with delight, looking straight at me. "Another passion of yours."

I found it odd that he said it more as a statement than a question. Was it that obvious just from me pronouncing the Japanese term? On the other hand, what else could he conclude when it had taken me to that faraway country several times?

"More so than food," I admitted. "I've been doing it since I was a teenager. That's over forty years."

"I guess you've been eating longer than that."

I had to smile.

"But not with the same passion."

That was certainly true. The moment I came across aikido, I knew I had to do it. Had to. And when I started to practice, I even dreamed about it frequently. Aikido occupied my mind all but completely. It was like I immediately knew I had found what I wanted to do for life. Passion might be an understatement.

Several decades later, it is easy to see how right I was about that first impression. All those years, aikido has continued to be a major ingredient in my life. There are not many things I hold on to that persistently. Not willingly, anyway.

"So, what is aikido to you?" Cael inquired.

"It's a Japanese martial art. The keyword is art. It's an

art. That's probably why I don't get bored with it, as I do with most things. We throw each other around, but what we really do is to explore just how far this strange dance can take us. How the strife for perfection can take you practically to the point of magic."

I found myself waving my hand, still holding the knife, in spiral patterns similar to those of aikido techniques. Cael was staring at it with an expression of fascination. I stopped.

What made me start with aikido was just that – a sense of magic. Back in my teens, a friend of mine had practiced aikido for a few years. Reluctantly, he showed me a technique that was little more than just waving the hand, but I fell to the floor as if clubbed down. Like magic. I had to learn it.

That friend of mine had practiced aikido, but kept it to himself. I had to drag it out of him. A teenage boy not bragging about knowing something as cool as an exotic martial art! In those days, few knew anything more about it than the fragments in some movies.

So, I persisted with my questions until he accepted to show me that one aikido technique. And I was hooked.

Also, the impression I got from aikido already at that first glimpse was so different from what one would think about a martial art. No attacks, no fight, no resistance. It was about blending with the attacker and effortlessly lead the aggression to a peaceful ending, enjoyable for both. It was turning a fight into a dance. What was not to love about that?

"Magic, you say."

"Well, the magic of any art. How a painting appears on white canvas, how a novel emerges from a white sheet of paper – or, nowadays, the blank area of a new word processor document on the computer screen. Writers talk about the curse of the white sheet. You can get stuck worrying about what could be significant and important enough to rightfully fill it. But once you get started, the text grows as if out of nowhere. Like magic."

"I have no problem with magic," Cael assured me. "Believe me. None at all." He had the perfect smile for his statement. It was neither so big it would indicate he was mocking me, nor so small it would look insincere. "So, what's the magic of aikido?"

"The transformation. An attack is turned into cooperation. The hard becomes soft, the force melts instantly into gentleness. It's about the mindset and not the physical action. Your attitude is irresistibly contagious. The attacker is transformed, as well as the attack. War is turned into peace."

As I spoke, I found that my hand had recommenced its dance in the air, though this time without the knife. It felt significantly better, so I let it go on until Cael spoke.

"How is that possible?"

Cael's question had no tone of dismissal. He genuinely wanted to know, as if already fully convinced it was somehow manageable. I paused shortly in search of the words that would pinpoint what I meant.

"It's in the attitude. If I genuinely keep a peaceful mind, the attacker's mind will transform into the same mindset upon contact. It's as irresistible as a catalyst."

"Why?"

I shrugged my shoulders.

"I wonder, too. That's the magic of it. Maybe it's simply because we all want to be peaceful, deep at heart. I just know that it only works if I'm completely sincere about it, and not trying to use it as a trick to win. When I do it for the joy of peace and nothing else, then it works. Otherwise not."

"Your conviction convinces the attacker?"

"That's what it feels like. Probably peace is the ultimate power. I'd like to think so."

"Yes, that would be nice."

I glanced at Cael. Was he ironic? I couldn't see it. His smile seemed nothing but gentle. But I had already come to realize that there was surely a lot more going on inside his head than what met the eyes.

"It would be fun to try," he added after a moment of silence.

Was he tempted to test me? That was not a rare occurrence when people inquired about aikido. Often, they would start to ooze of restrained aggression. It was as if they sought permission to be a little violent and thereby get some frustration out of their system. It could get awkward.

"Are you sure?" I asked with a grain of spice added to my voice. "I've done it quite a lot, you know."

His xylophone played, this time long enough to form a melody. I had to wait for it to end, unable to figure out exactly what caused it. But one thing was sure. He didn't feel the least bit intimidated. Did he also have a martial arts background?

He might be rather fit. It was hard to tell through his Armani suit. But he was quite slender and his features so delicate, much more like a lover than a fighter.

On the other hand, I was fully aware that looks can be deceptive. His straight posture, something sadly rare nowadays, suggested physical prowess. So did his elegant hand movements and the smooth way of walking I had observed earlier. It hit me that he could be a rock climber. That seemed also to fit his character.

He just kept on laughing.

*

When his laughter finally died out, I noticed that Cael still had not touched any of the caviar on his plate. It made me think that he was far more used to such extravagances than he admitted.

Well, he did say he was familiar with Russian caviar. Maybe he found this assortment mediocre in comparison. He would not be way off.

"You compared aikido to the arts," he said. "So, would you call yourself an artist at heart?"

"Definitely," I replied at once. "That's what makes me tick, no doubt. Already when I was a kid, what I really loved to do was write and make drawings. I did it all the time. Drawing came first, of course. But as soon as I got the hang of the alphabet, I started writing. Little stories that it's just as well I've forgotten. I wrote by hand at first. Then I learned to use my mom's typewriter. It was made for travel, with a case and a handle – but it was a big thing." I showed with my hands. "It weighed a ton. It felt like a great feat being able to use it. I went on to make school papers, which took hours and hours to print with the simple equipment at our disposal in school. God, the time I spent on that stuff!"

In my mind, I was back to those school duplicating machines, much more complicated than the photocopying that would later make them completely obsolete.

In middle school, making our class paper, I used the spirit duplicator our teachers were also utilizing. That was an invention from the 1920's. It allowed for colors, but the number of copies was limited to little more than a class set. The fumes of the alcohol, which gradually dissolved the wax colors, made me dizzy.

In high school I shifted to the mimeograph, because I was making school papers in hundreds of copies. I doubt that the chemicals of its ink were any healthier than the alcohol of its predecessor. And it only printed in black.

Where did I get the persistence to struggle with them so much, and for so long? I could have been out playing with the other kids – or, later, trying to get myself laid. But I persisted with that stuff all through high school. Something urged me on. I still don't know exactly what. But sure enough, my adult life has been one of journalism as well as writing books. The printed word had me captured, much like aikido.

"I continued to write stories for those school papers or just as school assignments," I explained to Cael. "Not until I was twenty-two did I write my first novel. The first version of it was nineteen pages. When I rewrote it, it swelled to ninety. At next rewrite it was doubled. Then I wrote another novel, and another, feverishly. I had found my calling."

"So, you're a writer."

"Yes, but not at all a famous one. You surely haven't come across any of my books. Also, for a long time they were only in Swedish. It's just these last few years I've been writing in English."

"How about drawing? Did you drop that?"

"Actually, I concentrated on painting before writing my first novel. I even had a couple of exhibitions in the area where I lived back then. But the gallery world, it wasn't my thing. People drinking white wine and calling each other darling."

I could feel my face form a bitter expression, as if I had taken a bite on a lemon. Memories of uncomfortable gallery visits back in the 1970's flashed through my mind, but I brushed them off.

"In those days, galleries were the only way an artist could bring his work to the public. A very select part of the public, unfortunately. By time, it disgusted me. I had to do something else. Then I came up with the idea for a novel, and that was it."

*

I had no intention at all of telling Cael what that idea was, but my first novel started with a sentence forming in my head. It was the beginning of the story. Here it is in English:

> *Sunshine caressed Tristan's face, his forehead, cheeks and lips.*

The chapter went on describing Tristan, a boy in his late teens, relaxing on a rock right by the water. The rays of the summer sun convinced him to undress and splash water from the lake onto his skin to cool down. That in turn tickled him into an erection, and he masturbated.

Nothing odd about that. He had a sweet moment of self-indulgence, with its natural conclusion. I used this opening scene to describe his mentality, which was one of unconcealed hedonism.

The title of the novel was *Tristan's Karma*, by which I implied the nature of young love. Tristan without any specific Iseult. A love not directed towards another, but a personal thing.

Adolescents lovs to love, whatever the object. They get drunken on their own emotion. Sort of like Baudelaire suggests in his famous poem *Be Drunken*, "On wine, on poetry or on virtue as you wish." Of course, the young will first of all be drunken on love.

Well, some would call it lust.

When teens make love, it is really an act of mutual masturbation. The fire in their loins is ignited and they search desperately for a distinguisher.

On the other hand, that mutual masturbation might to a large extent also be true for adults. We do what we need to get by. But adolescence, in particular, is quite a tribulation.

That first novel of mine is still unpublished. I have not been totally eager to make it happen. Much like just about every writer's career starts, it is a coming-of-age story. But I had exposed some aching personal sentiments when writing it – as one should, mind you. But there you go. Just thinking about it still makes me uneasy.

My main character Tristan was inspired by a friend I had back then. He was a veritable Narcissus, immensely attractive to the eye as well as the heart. I loved him. We all did, everyone who knew him. But he was, in a way, completely enclosed in his own delight. Unreachable on top of that pedestal that we helped him erect.

At least, that was how it felt to me. I might have been unfair in my judgment of him.

Anyway, some years later he happened to end up much the same way as I had Tristan's story end. And I knew it, long before it happened. That didn't make it hurt any less.

So, I'm in no hurry to get the book published. I quickly wrote others that were.

But I know my mind well enough to accept that an unpublished story will continue to haunt my thoughts and influence every book I write, in one way or other. There is but one way to get it out of my system, and that is to have it published and thereby be gone.

"What was it about?" Cael wondered, interrupting my flow of memories.

"What was what about?" I asked, confused as if snapped out of a daydream. Well, that was pretty much the case. "My first book?"

He nodded patiently.

"Oh, it was just a coming-of-age thing. Isn't that what every young writer starts with?"

Cael shrugged his shoulders.

"You tell me," he said.

Something about his voice made me wonder what he implied. I told myself I was being ridiculous.

*

I felt increasingly awkward, but the relief came quickly. Cael had another question for me.

"How about your painting?"

That rascal had hit another nerve. Were it not for his charm and exceptionally good looks, I would have searched for the nearest exit.

I love painting. But I don't do it. That's as frustrating as it sounds. It is strange that I haven't pursued it more, since painting feels so much more rewarding to me than writing. I have no idea why.

When I'm in a particularly solemn mode, I say to people that writing is talking to people, and painting is talking to the gods. I know it's over the top, but that's what it feels like to me.

Still, I haven't done it much since I started writing books in the mid-1970's.

It's not that writing takes all of my time. Except for short periods of obsession when writing a new story, I can easily make time – plenty of time – for other activities. Then I return to my story without any problem. If weeks or months have passed, I need to reread the script to get back into it, but that's quickly done.

The problem is that painting takes time. A lot of time. And it demands exclusive access to my attention.

When I paint, really paint, I get into kind of a trance. Hours fly by. Soon, so do days and weeks. There is no opening to sit down for a few hours work on a manuscript. I hardly find time to do regular household chores. Sometimes

I even forget about eating, until I get dizzy from low blood sugar.

Also, there is what I call a warm-up period needed for painting. When I write, I can do so now and then in an irregular fashion, and still the words flow as they should on my keyboard. Not so with painting.

I have to get really into it for a week or more, before the result on the canvas is the least bit satisfactory. Already the charcoal sketch on the canvas is nothing but doodle, until I have spent the time needed to be absorbed.

Maybe it has something to do with the skill of the hand needed to draw as well as paint. That skill may be latent, but some time is needed to wake it up after a long period of absence from the exercise.

Much to my frustration, painting can't be a part-time job. It is like a stern marriage, allowing no mistresses. Not even casual flirts.

So, since the 70's I have been longing for the opportunity to return to painting full time. It has become my dream for the future. What I will do when I grow up. I still haven't grown up.

I have tried painting a number of times since back then. But unable to give it all the time needed, the results just left me disappointed. I stored away the easel and returned to the keyboard.

I have not given it up. Someday I will take the time. How I look forward to it! Again, I don't really know why. But I do.

"I still paint, now and then," I explained to Cael. I could hear the melancholy tone of my voice. "There are long intervals in between. Very long. I miss it and always tell myself I'll return to it, one of these days. But you know how those things go, if that day isn't today."

"Isn't every day today?"

I had to smile, though Cael seemed quite serious.

"There's no denying that," I admitted. "And I don't worry too much, since I can feel I have a bunch of paintings inside of me. They will demand to come out."

I could say that with true conviction. One of these days. Absolutely.

"Is that how it works with your books, too? They are already inside you, urging you to let them out?"

"Pretty much. It's not that I know what they are, except for some very vague ideas, but I know when one pops up and charges forward. And I bet I will know when there is no more book waiting inside of me, when I've written the last one."

"It sounds like you long for it."

"I'm in no hurry," I said with a chuckle that came out with a rather hollow sound. "I'm not even sure it will happen. But if it does, I will know it."

"That one, at least, I must read," Cael said, adding a little smile but sounding very determined.

"Don't hold your breath," I replied.

Time for the Caviar

At that moment I realized we had talked about me almost exclusively. I had talked about me. That's something I rarely do. Instead, I love to do what Cael seemed to be doing right now – explore the psyche of the person in front of me with a series of questions, gradually getting more personal, more at depth.

He was doing my thing. And I had complied, without any hesitation.

I'm not that comfortable talking about myself. That's rather unfair of me, considering how I enjoy having others go on about themselves, as long as they do so according to my curiosity, my line of questioning. At the rare occasions I talk about me, I'm embarrassed to admit even to myself, it doesn't take long before I start to feel like bragging. That happens whatever it is I say about myself.

I feel as if making myself important. Special, as the Americans love to put it – a word I find ridiculous. Isn't everything special? Everything or nothing. In my case, I know that I am amazed by what goes on inside my head. It is probably to what I devote just about all my life. But that doesn't stop me from being almost nauseated by flaunting it, when talking about myself.

It could be an example of what we Scandinavians call the Jante Law, an observation first made by the Norwegian author Aksel Sandemose. The law states: Don't think you are somebody, don't think you matter, and so on. The law of self-denial, being quite a force in Scandinavian society.

My variation of it is that I am fine with having enormous self-esteem, but I should keep it to myself.

I guess I learned that lesson already as a little schoolboy. In the classroom, any tendency to stand out was viciously attacked by the others, like a pack of wolves. So I mostly did my best to hide what talent I had, not unlike the secrecy when working as a restaurant critic.

"But enough about me," I said, without meeting Cael's eyes, so as not to be too forward. "Now, let's talk about you."

"We will get to that," Cael replied matter-of-factly. "There's still plenty of time."

As a reflex, I glanced at that giant clock in the lobby, surrounded by buffet tables. As far as I could see, it was no more than twenty past eleven. Had we only been here for twenty minutes? I checked my cell phone. It showed the same.

That surprised me, but I didn't think too much of it. I have always been lousy at keeping track of time. Not just minutes and hours, but days and months, even years. I just forget about them, if not constantly reminded.

When I was a kid asking my mother what day it was, she would tell me, "You're not at school and all the stores are closed. What day can it be?" Back then, we went to school also on Saturdays, so I concluded that it must be Sunday. But it took me a while.

I'm still the same. If I didn't have aikido classes at certain weekdays, I would quickly mess it all up.

"Time is relative, you know," Cael said. "We'll get the time we need."

*

"Now, let's not forget about the caviar," Cael continued, looking down at his plate. "How do you suggest we do this?"

I took the opportunity to fill our glasses. I noticed that there wasn't much Champagne remaining in the bottle.

"First things first," I said with a smile and raised my glass.

We had the glasses clash, slightly more distinctly than the first time, but we said nothing. After a generous sip of it, I continued.

"Let's start with the trout roe, since it's as close to salmon as we get here. I'd say it should be enjoyed as is, at least to begin with." I picked some of it up with my fork. "Already looking at it is quite a treat. Something from a treasure chamber."

We did so for a moment.

"On the tongue, I love to pop those little marbles against the roof of my mouth. It's quite a sensation."

We did that. Cael had an expression of amazement as he closed his mouth and let his tongue do its work. It was clear that he enjoyed this just as much as I did.

The taste was distinctly marine, even intrusively so. It was not exactly tasty, but it had authority. Also the surface of the roe was quite firm, needing some force to be popped by the tongue. So, both its flavor and its taste were rather tough. I thought that it was a little bit rude for the Champagne. Vodka would probably work better. And some crème fraîche would bring it down a notch.

"How could you ever quit as a restaurant critic?" Cael wondered when he had swallowed the trout roe.

"I can still have this. Actually, I can have what I like. As a critic, you don't go around picking your favorite food. If you do the job seriously, you must first of all try the food that the restaurant presents as its signature dishes, whatever your own preferences may be. And you can't write like I've spoken so far, specifying how you want it. You must try their way with an open mind."

"Maybe you took the job too seriously," he commented with a quick grin.

"Probably. But I wasn't that very disciplined. If they served scallops or duck liver or other favorites of mine, I would tend to choose those dishes even when it was obvious that the restaurant was the most proud of other ones. God forgive me."

"I'm sure he does."

"Now you tell me, how did you like the trout roe?"

Cael took another sample of it, before replying. That impressed me. There's a distinct difference between tasting something and doing it to say something about it.

"It's fun, no doubt," he said after a pensive moment. "But there is a liveliness missing in it. It's like it knows too well that it will never turn into a trout."

I could feel my eyes widen. That was the kind of expression I might have used. I hurried to taste some more of it.

"I see what you mean," I said, still with the roe in my mouth, exploring it with my tongue. "It has passed its prime, minutely. I think you could do my job."

"You're too kind," he said. "I was just trying to be you."

"I don't know if I should be flattered, or disturbed because it was so easy for you."

We both kind of chuckled, but at least on my part it was a little bit strained.

"Let's move on to the other caviars," Cael suggested.

I was happy to do so. On my suggestion, we went for the bright yellow whitefish caviar. The moment it entered my mouth, it brought the scent of a lake, reminding me of youthful nocturnal swimming in the nude with giggling friends. That was nice, of course.

At first, we tasted it without any accoutrement. Then we decided to add it to one of the small blinis, together with crème fraîche and some chopped chives. I waited for Cael's reaction.

"I don't know," he said. "It's nice, no doubt, but not at all the sensation we had with the trout roe."

"I agree. Pleasant but not a lasting experience. The tiny roe grains tumble around on the tongue in a joyful dance, kind of a game of tag. But the taste is as elusive as the winner of that game needs to be. And I'm not at all sure about the chives with any kind of caviar. They're sort of aiming in the opposite direction."

"You didn't even get any shallot."

"I can't imagine that it would do a better job with caviar than simple yellow onion. Shallot is for cooking. To me, the best one with caviar of just about any kind is the red onion."

"We've got that on our plates."

On the next blini, he tried the whitefish caviar with red onion on top of the crème fraîche. I didn't bother to do the same.

"Slightly better," he said while still chewing on it. "But still far from the experience with the trout roe."

We handled the brightly colored Tobiko flying fish caviar just as briefly. Its saltiness was rather simple, as was its slight marine scent. Like the herring roe, its forte was the crunchy texture.

After washing it down with Champagne, we turned our attention to the glossy grayish paddlefish roe. Quite elaborately, we prepared our blinis with crème fraîche.

"Let's skip the onion," I suggested, having tasted the caviar on its own previously.

Cael nodded, showing a happy face, almost like a child in an amusement park. Both of us took the blini in one bite, and then slowly chewed on it for a while in silence.

"That's more like it," I said after finally swallowing. "This is caviar, albeit not an imperial one. It's soft and buttery, with an intriguing aftertaste. Compared to its nobler relatives, though, it leaves less of an impression. One has to forget about them in order to enjoy this one fully."

"There wasn't much of a pop," Cael complained, looking rather disappointed. "But it blends quite well with the blini and the crème fraîche."

We prepared a second blini, exactly the same.

"I agree with you that there's no need for onion," Cael said as he was working on his blini. "I've also noticed that you haven't used lemon on anything so far."

"It's used far too much," I replied, shaking my head. "Lemon is so poignant, it should be treated with great care. For example, when I add it to a white meat fish, it's only when I've eaten so much of it that I need some variation. Not from the start. Lemon kills subtle flavors. It even interferes with your sense of the texture, because it makes your mouth contract. With caviar, I would say it's only useful if the caviar is a disappointment."

"That's not the case here."

"It isn't. Not that this thing compares to Beluga in the least. The aftertaste is too short and the sophistication is far from as complex. But it doesn't need any distinct additional flavors to justify its existence."

Cael nodded, preparing his next blini the same way.

"Now, the question is," I continued, keeping my eyes on him, "how does it compare to the trout roe?"

Cael looked up from his plate, slightly surprised and intrigued.

"You're asking me?"

I nodded. He let the blini rest on his plate, although it was ready to be consumed. He was silent for quite long, before replying.

"I'd say that this caviar is superior, but only because the trout roe was not vibrantly fresh. If it had been, there would have been no contest. The popping and liveliness of the trout roe is so much more invigorating than the somber dark paddlefish caviar. They are almost opposites. Light and dark, life and death. Not that death is only malicious, but life is..."

"Yes?"

Cael let go of his utensils, leaning back in the chair.

"Life is," he stated with a sudden gravity in his voice, looking straight at me. "Death is not."

That, I had to think about. I even said it:

"I have to think about that."

"Be my guest," Cael replied with a delightful little smile.

"You said it so firmly. Do you think that there is no death?"

"Or there is nothing after death. How can its taste surpass that of life, which is definitely something?"

"Which one is it?"

"How would I know?"

He broke into that delightful xylophone laughter. I did the same, although with much less of a musical flair. And I was louder.

Evasive Love

Cael poured what little was left of the Champagne into our glasses. He raised his.

"To life!" he said.

I just nodded as we emptied the glasses. Then we stood up and grabbed our plates to refill on the caviar. We agreed to make it only paddlefish and trout.

"Let's continue with the crème fraîche," I suggested. "And maybe we should add some shrimps, just to see how that works out?"

On the way to the buffet, we passed our waiter. I was quick to order another bottle of Champagne.

"This one's on me," I said to Cael.

"Why, thank you," he replied with a charming expression of delight passing over his face.

"Please," I urged him.

Normally I have the habit of responding with a thank you to any thank you. I like the politeness of it, contrary to "you're welcome," which seems much less modest in sort of confirming that there was something for which to be thankful. That is kind of rude, like giving with one hand and taking back with the other. I guess my "please," popping out of me involuntarily, was sort of the same as thanking for thanks, with additional emphasis.

Courtesy is a maze, but it is worth exploring.

Again I thought of Kurt Vonnegut, who quoted a fan of his in the prologue to the novel *Jailbird*. This fan, a high-school student, had come to the conclusion that all his novels could be summed up to one single idea: Love may fail, but courtesy will prevail. Vonnegut confessed that the student might be right.

We reached the caviar table and allowed ourselves quite generous portions from it. After adding a handful of shrimps, and – with some hesitation – a lobster tail and claw, our plates were rather full. Just as Cael gently put a lobster claw on his plate, seeming to be completely occupied by that task, he said with a very soft voice, little more than a whisper:

"Don't give up on love just yet, Stefan."

It startled me as much as if he had suddenly shouted "Boo!" I stared at him.

"I'm sorry if I was getting too personal," he said.

"Not at all," I said, though still not having decided on the issue. "What made you say it?"

He shrugged his shoulders.

"Could it have been your 'please' just now?" he suggested, as if it was a mystery to him, too. He turned and started for our table, before I had time to respond.

I stood still and looked at his back while he walked the first few steps. Had I accidentally been thinking out loud? Had I mumbled the Vonnegut quote, unawares? I didn't think so, but I was not completely sure. Or had he simply spotted the sadness that sometimes surfaces on my face, when I get lost in my own thoughts?

I decided to just shrug it off.

*

Still, when we were seated at our table and the waiter filled our glasses from the second bottle of Champagne, I returned to the subject.

"I don't really believe in it," I said.

"In what?" he asked, although I had no doubt he knew what I meant. He was probably just being gentle.

"In love. I suspect it's mainly a cultural thing, a social behavior with other forces behind it."

"So you'd agree with Vonnegut?"

Aha, I thought. I had been thinking aloud. Although that bothered me, especially since I had not been aware of it, I still relaxed. Mystery solved.

"I believe in lust," I went on. "In affection, too. The need for companions, the comfort of another person's touch, the fear of losing someone dear, the urge to reproduce. All those things and more. I just don't think love exists, at least not the way it is presented in matrimony, in poetry and all those Hollywood movies with happy endings."

"Maybe you're just not the sentimental type?"

"Oh, I'm ridiculously sentimental! I weep at the end of those silly Hollywood movies. Not in some joy of their happily ever after, but because of the fiction of it. That's just not how it goes. Love is an illusion, though sometimes mutual. A dream from which everyone wakes up, sooner or later. The absurdity is evident in the marriage vows. How can you promise to love your spouse until death do you apart? It's like they try to make it so by some magic spell. That's why they need a church to do it in, a place of worship of metaphysical forces."

As I was talking, Cael's smile was slowly widening. He ended with a short laugh.

"It's a good thing this food is already cold," he said and pointed to his plate.

"I'm sorry."

He just waved my excuse off.

"I'm sure the lobster will gain flavor from getting closer to room temperature. And I find what you say interesting. Almost everyone says that love is the meaning of life, the one thing that mankind never can have too much of and cannot live without."

I shrugged my shoulders.

"The only thing I see is how people frantically cling to this illusion. Often enough, it ruins their lives instead of fulfilling them."

"What about 'Tis better to have loved and lost, than never to have loved at all'?"

"Tennyson wrote that about a friend who died, not a lover. I believe in friendship. Very much so. Without friends, we succumb. And it's hard not to succumb when they do."

I had a memory flash of a close aikido friend who passed away many years ago, as I always do when a subject of this kind comes up. His demise was not completely unexpected, but still impossible for me to get over. I had to blink.

"Of course," I resumed, "lovers can be friends, too, though usually not for that long. What they believe to be their love is what messes it up."

"So, you believe in Agape, but not Eros?"

"Oh, I believe in Eros, the archetype of lust. I would be a fool to deny it. Actually, I also believe that there is a very fine line between Eros and Agape, between lust and friendship. One easily leads to the other, if we let it. Maybe we should."

I halted myself, feeling my cheeks burn. I had slipped into getting more personal than I had intended. Life had taught me, in several severe lessons, not to speak my mind out loud on just any issue. There is so much sacred or even taboo. We may all think it, but we are not to say it. I usually stick to that, although never really accepting it.

Cael's smile was on the verge of becoming a laugh. He tilted his head to the side.

"I don't judge," he said. "I observe, I reflect, sometimes I interfere. But I never judge."

His words and his gaze made me blush even more, but somehow I still relaxed. I had no idea why he said what he did, but his words were strangely comforting, nonetheless. I continued.

"I can celebrate when people say they are in love and act upon it. I wish them luck and hope it lasts. But I don't believe it does. Myself, I have not been able to fall in love more than briefly, and just a few times."

"And how did that feel, while it lasted?"

"Frustrating."

Now, he laughed. I couldn't, but my lips twitched in the effort of a smile. We started digging into the caviar.

*

I have loved, of course, but I can't say I have liked it. It's not only that love hurts, as the song says. More frustrating is that it doesn't satisfy. It can't. Not me, anyway, but I have come to the firm conviction that it goes for everyone, whatever they claim.

I've heard I don't know how many couples assure me that this was the real thing, a symbiosis perfecting both their lives, keeping them in a petrified state of bliss, and so on. Upon scrutiny, though, I have seen their anguish, their continued thirst, their ambiguity, their growing displeasure. They were trying to convince themselves, which worked fine for a while – but never at length.

Those who have stayed together the longest seem to be the ones with the least illusions about their love. They have learned to accept the limits of what love can give.

What binds them together as couples is convenience, more than anything else. A partner with whom to share the daily chores. Regularly accessible sex without the complications of seduction. The security of having someone else looking after you. Company as a mutual shield against solitude. What it boils down to is convenience.

But I can see the longing in their eyes. They never stop wishing for something more. Society tends to glorify love, the kind that is supposed to glue two persons together so tightly, it could be described as fusion. With the same temperature rise. But that is a cultural norm, little more than a myth. It conforms to social expectations and demands, much more than to human feelings. We pretend it is true, just to fulfill what we perceive to be the social contract.

Without the expectation preached to us practically from birth, I doubt that we would at all bother to form couples – at least not for more than very brief periods of time. Fidelity is just not in us.

Well, we can be faithful for a while, as long as no one else tempts us more. That's not fidelity. It's opportunity.

I explained that to a friend, years ago. He and his lover had an open relationship. They were free to sleep around, because they were convinced that they would never break up. After an amorous adventure, they would always find their way back to each other.

I told him that this would only last until someone else came along, sweeping him off his feet. It would never happen, he assured me with a conviction I found kind of cute.

Just a month after that conversation, it happened. He met someone else, and the open relationship ended abruptly, replaced by one with much more commitment.

His deserted lover was devastated. He had also believed their bond was unbreakable. And there he was, suddenly alone. Love is merciless.

I have also known couples who made even me believe that they would last forever. Matches made in heaven. Some of them are still together, but most of them are not. The odds speak loud and clear.

One friend had a wife who was an absolutely ravishing beauty. Like a movie star, yet warm and down to earth. They sure seemed happy together. We all envied them. Until he suddenly divorced her, seemingly out of the blue.

It would have been easier to understand the opposite, but he was the one breaking it up. When I asked him about it, I didn't have to say very much before he interrupted me by explaining, "Beauty is not enough."

Nothing is enough, at length.

Usually I find that there is a cruel math to relationships. If both don't crave each other exactly as much, it is doomed. The inequality is a crack, rapidly widening. That happens even if the difference is minute. The exact balance needed is almost impossible to find – and to keep.

Another decisive factor, which seems like a vicious joke of nature, is that of self-esteem, or rather the lack thereof. Many a lover wrestles with this flawed reasoning, and looses to it: If the partner settled for someone as petty as him or her, then how petty must that partner be? It seems absurd, but I have seen it so often. We are our own worst enemies.

Me, I have certainly destroyed several relationships by my disbelief in them. I tended to do so even before I had reached that conclusion. I am definitely not the marrying kind. I would be a hypocrite to try it.

Still, I admit I have tried. Well, not marriage, but similar commitments without the vows. I might do so again, though surely not with much hope. And without hope, what are the chances of success?

The trap that gets me every time is one and the same. I fall for beauty. Who doesn't? Granted, beauty comes in many shapes and forms, but in every case it does the trick. When it appears in abundance, beauty immediately makes me fall in love.

I always make the mistake of thinking it is the person I fall in love with, but I really know it is not. It's the beauty, of whatever kind. Like an object of art. Probably, it is not really love I feel, but admiration. Sometimes veneration, like of something sacred. And yes, beauty is something divine.

So, at the most it is a question of worship. One should not try to love what one worships. That leads to disaster.

Yet, when beauty enters the stage, who remembers to be cautious?

*

"How about you, Cael?" I resumed after having some caviar, accompanied by shrimps. "Don't leave me stranded here. I practically spilled my guts, just now."

"Oh, there's more to you," he said with conviction. "Much more."

"But now it's your turn."

He paused with the eating, but held on to his knife and fork.

"I can tell you this about love, which is the same as with so many other things: If you feel it, if you are convinced of it – no matter how briefly – is it not real?"

I opened my mouth to reply, but he didn't let me.

"The names we put on things are not the things we put them on."

His words both surprised and amused me.

"That's something I could have said. Are you a Taoist, perchance?" I quoted the *Tao Te Ching*, "There are already many names. One must know when it is enough."

He replied immediately:

"The name that can be named is not the eternal name."

"How about that!" I exclaimed with great delight. "Is it by any chance my translation you quote? I think several translations have the same wording for that line in the first chapter of the Tao Te Ching, and so does mine. On other lines, though, we differ quite a lot."

"The way that can be walked is not the eternal way," Cael added.

"Yes, that's definitely my translation!" I was delighted. Someone quoting a book of mine was not an experience to which I had become accustomed, especially not outside Sweden. "Most of them keep the Chinese word Tao and therefore tend to interpret it, 'the Tao that can be told.' But Tao, the Way, is both a noun and a verb. The Way and walking it. Lao Tzu made a joke. His Way is another than the one you walk to get from one place to another. You've read my book?"

"It's on the internet," Cael replied, amused by my sudden enthusiasm. He was pleased, too, it seemed.

"I could talk for hours about Lao Tzu and his text, but let's not forget that it's about you, now. Do you believe in love?"

His smile was replaced by an expression getting close to sadness.

"Sorry to disappoint you, but yes." He waited a moment for me to ponder his answer, before he continued, "What's more, so do you."

My eyebrows curved and struggled to meet above my nose. His smile did not return, although I probably looked rather funny in my confusion.

I wanted to object, but my confusion made me dumb. Me believe in love?

I didn't even like the word – well, in English. It is short, and it's both a verb and a noun, so people say it far too often, diluting it of any sincerity or profound meaning. In the English language it has become as common and bland as if it were a preposition.

Swedish, my native tongue, is different. The noun is *kärlek*, which is a compound word, meaning 'dear game,' as if but a careless amusement played by childish minds. Sweet and pleasant.

The verb is *älska*, an old word with a different etymology. It just means what it means, but it sounds so much more attractive than the English counterpart. It starts with an open and inviting vowel, sounding sort of like the 'a' in 'any.' As one's tongue moves from 'l' to 's' it feels like preparing for cunnilingus. The short and rather hard 'ka' at the end is where the action begins.

The word is also used for the act of making love, of course, but it brings this sensation to every use of the word. It is very erotic in nature, when pronounced, whereas 'love' is plump, as sudden and disappointing as premature ejaculation.

The old traditional Swedish noun for intercourse, sadly not much in use anymore, is *älskog*. The 'o' is long and rich, sort of like in 'who,' and the 'g' forms a very gentle ending, as if urging us to continue forever. It's a word for making life one of making love.

"You are indeed a man of letters," Cael interrupted my thoughts and smiled sort of graciously.

I found myself blushing. Thinking of the mere words – in Swedish – had made my temperature rise, also in my groin. I had no idea of what his comment referred to, since he was the one speaking also before that remark. But I was happy to snap out of thoughts that were about to arouse me beyond my ability to hide it.

"Love is a word, as we have both stated," Cael continued. "Some of the definitions floating around in society might be way off. Surely. Others are absolutely absurd. But there is something behind it, something real and utterly powerful."

He raised his index finger, which made him look like Leonardo da Vinci's last painting, portraying John the Baptist pointing sort of seductively towards heaven.

I knew that painting very well, and loved it. I'd even seen it at the Louvre museum in Paris. One could step right up to it, even touch it if one dared, contrary to how extremely protected *La Gioconda*, the Mona Lisa, was at the same museum. John's gesture and smile suggested high and low at the same time – sanctity and sin. The one cannot exist without the other.

I had made my own version of that painting, when I started getting serious with oil on canvas in my early twenties. I had to, although I knew that there was nothing I could add to Leonardo's original. It was a fan painting of sorts. Homage. I was a huge fan. I still am.

Looking right at Cael and his gesture, I realized that in my eyes he now looked exactly like that Leonardo painting, as if John had appeared in front of me, taking Cael's place. Bare chest and all.

I had to blink hard a couple of times, before I saw Cael in his white shirt and black suit again.

That was no shock to me, at all. My eyes had played such tricks on me before, when I reminisced or wandered off in daydreams. Once, I had even seen another face on someone I was making love to at the time – actually the face of the person I would have wanted there instead. It was so clear, that other face, I stopped momentarily in complete amazement.

Of course, I kept it to myself.

My thoughts were interrupted by Cael bursting into one of his xylophone laughs. He dropped his hand.

"What?" I asked.

He shook his head, still smiling.

"That something behind the word love," he continued

his explanation, "is what all the emotions you mentioned before have in common. So, it's not that love doesn't exist while the other feelings do. They are all the same, essentially, and love is as good a name as any for it."

I was not sure that he had convinced me, but I was moved by the beauty of the words – in combination with the beauty of the one who uttered them.

We were silent for quite a while, not even eating. We just looked at each other. It was peaceful. The noise around us got muffled, as if coming from a stereo on which the volume was lowered.

"So, have you loved?" I finally managed to ask, sort of breaking the spell. The noise around us returned. "With your looks, I can't imagine that you haven't had plenty of opportunities."

"All the time." He repeated, with emphasis on both words and pausing slightly between them, "All time."

Then he laughed and refilled our glasses.

Elusive Life

I wouldn't mind at all listening to some of Cael's love stories, but I was not about to ask him. Nor did he seem inclined to tell me. He was happily devouring the rest of the caviar, the shrimps and the lobster. I was a bit more careful, since there was quite a lot yet to explore at the buffet.

Instead, I sipped calmly on the Champagne, having a look around at the other brunch guests of the Peacock Alley.

There were quite a lot of them, although several tables were still vacant. Some of the guests were dressed up, as if going to church or the theater. Others were not. Most of them were properly dressed, but nothing fancy.

I remembered some statement about a dress code for the Sunday brunch, but apparently it was nothing the staff pursued vigorously. My tie could stay rolled up in my pocket.

I had all but forgotten about the piano player. Now, I listened and heard him more clearly.

He had the discretion of allowing brunch guests to simply forget about his presence, should they prefer that. It was almost as if he performed in a library. He sang, too, into a microphone, but his voice was rather mellow and the speakers were not that loud. Just so that his voice was not drowned by the sound from the grand piano, which he played quite gently.

His repertoire was the usual one of neutrally performed evergreens and contemporary pop songs from high up on the charts. Not that very far from elevator music. I let my ears lose their attention to it.

Then I became aware that Cael had just said something. I turned to him.

"Sorry, I didn't hear."

"Were you listening to the piano player?"

"Not really. He is playing background music, which is quite enough here."

Cael sent a quick glance in the direction of the piano player. Then his eyes were back on me.

"I was asking what makes you happy. It's not love, we have established. Something else, then?"

I looked at his face, which was expressing mild curiosity. It struck me that he no longer looked that much like Ezra Miller as I had marveled at to begin with. The dark Asian eyes were still there, as well as the pale skin and the black hair. But something in my perception of his face had changed. His features remained ravishing, but in their own way and not as a copy of someone else.

I thought the change was simply because I had gotten to know that face. It was no longer a stranger, and therefore Cael looked like no other than himself.

"Actually," I told him, "I don't really believe in happiness, either."

*

Of course, I have felt happy at times. Countless times. The moment that popped up from my memory was from childhood. An unforgettable though rather commonplace experience.

I was about nine or ten years old, living in the Stockholm suburb Hässelby. On the way by foot from my home to the shopping center, a distance not even reaching a mile, I changed from walking to skipping. It was on an impulse, just as I reached an overpass.

I crossed the overpass in no time, and it hit me that this hopping style of running was not only quite fast, but also completely effortless. It was as if I just sailed ahead, although there was not even any wind. As if gravity suddenly shifted to a forward instead of downward pull. I felt I could do it forever.

In my mind, it was like flying. The weight of the world disappeared.

I was overcome by happiness, so intense it would be more accurate to call it euphoria. There was something so joyous about the ease by which I skipped my way forward, I could have burst out laughing if I wasn't already consumed by the sensation and my speedy advance.

It was so fast I felt the resistance of the air as I plowed through it. I thought that this is how we should always transport ourselves. Skipping through life. We would never be sad.

When I reached the shopping center, I had to slow down to walking. But that did not put an end to my joy. It kept tickling all through my body. I had discovered something of immense value, which I could utilize at will, any time I wanted. I had found the panacea, the miracle cure for everything.

I marveled at nobody else seeming to know, although it was so obvious. What clouded their eyes? Or were they opposed to this instant kind of bliss, for some reason?

People did seem reluctant to have fun and feel good, for sure. Especially adults, but also kids of my own age. As if it were a sin. Already at that young age I had come across it more than once – the joy of one was the aggravation of the others. Those who did not laugh with you tended to scold you or even pick fights with you. Joy was met with anger. Strange.

It didn't always happen. I had also found laughter to

be contagious. But it was not a sure thing. Suddenly, people would be provoked by laughter, even though it was obvious that nobody laughed at them.

My conclusion was that people don't always want to be happy. Usually they don't. I had no idea why, but a child must learn the safe path through life. After all, man is a predator, also of other men.

So, I decided to keep the joy of skipping to myself, and to use this miracle cure with caution.

Now and then, I would start to skip, but only when I had no company and not for long. As the years passed, those moments became increasingly rare. I don't even remember the last time I did it.

*

Cael had been silent while I was reminiscing. He looked at me with his head tilted to the side and his lips closed in the faintest suggestion of a smile. It looked like pity.

"You are a hard man to please," he said.

I shrugged my shoulders. My hand went for the glass and I had another sip of the Champagne.

"It gets me thinking," Cael continued. "What's your meaning of life, if you have one?"

"My meaning of life?"

Cael nodded, with a tiny smile playing on his lips. He was still absolutely charming, indeed. I wanted to give him the best answer I could.

"I'd hesitate to speculate about one meaning of life applicable to all humans. I seriously doubt that there is such a thing."

"Right," he butted in. "That would be boring."

I was puzzled by his sudden statement, as if this was a quiz and he was the game leader with all the right answers.

This young man, what could he know about the meaning of life? I pretended not to have heard his remark, and continued.

"For me, I guess the closest I have gotten to a meaning is to explore all of what I might be able to express. My talents, if you will. After all, that's what I've been spending most of my time on. I'm doing an excavation of my mind, bringing out what treasures I find."

I sort of chuckled from sudden embarrassment.

"Treasures to me, anyway," I added. "That's the only criterion I can trust, the only one I feel satisfied with."

"Fine with me," Cael said. It seemed he did not subscribe to the Jante law of self-denial. "Please go on."

"The Japanese concept Do, the Way, is different from the Taoist version, although it's the same word. In everyday use, like in the word aikido, it signifies the personal path one chooses, by which to mature and realize oneself, refine one's abilities and character. They see it as the thing you do in order to work on and express your progress through life. Your vessel, so to speak. That's sort of what I do, and not only in my aikido practice. I strive to get as much as possible out of me, to discover what's inside of me."

"And what is that?"

"It's an ongoing process," I replied with a smile.

"Towards enlightenment?"

"Not really. I'm not even fond of that expression. I prefer satori, the Zen concept."

"But doesn't that word mean enlightenment?"

"That's how it's usually translated, but it's misleading. Satori is a passing thing, not a state you reach to remain there forever on. Suddenly, you have a kind of epiphany, where you grasp the essence and meaning of it all. Then you just go back to the same old same old. It will be different from that moment on, but you don't levitate away from it. The world is still there. It just becomes even more real, more worldly, than ever before."

I had one of those satori moments after three years of aikido, when I started throwing people without touching them and things like that. It was quite a sensation. But soon, I found myself continuing with the basic techniques in a regular fashion. They felt different, more refined or maybe simplified, but they didn't look much different.

Still, I was convinced it was a turning point. Something had changed. I had. But aikido had not, so I just continued with the practice.

After twelve years of training, I had another satori experience. It was less spectacular, but it probably changed the nature of my aikido even more. Things fell into place. My movements became part of me.

Also, I had a strong sense of realizing the role of aikido in my life. It was kind of like new shoes, when you break them in and stop noticing that you have them on. Aikido became a part of me, as natural as my skin and my breathing.

And I just kept practicing. I like that. You go on with life as usual, whatever you find on the way. There is a definite change, a spectacular one, but you go on almost like there wasn't one.

"By remaining in the world as we know it," I explained to Cael, "we notice that change much more than we would if we just escaped to some Nirvana or Paradise or whatever. I think the whole trick is not to go beyond reality, but to discover what reality really is."

"So, what is it?"

"That's what I strive to find out." I thought about my words for a while, and then I added, "What reality is to me. What my mind can tell me about reality."

"Any clues so far?" Cael inquired with a tone that could be ironic.

"Plenty. I just haven't connected them all, yet."

"You will." The irony was gone.

"That's what I keep thinking. Suddenly, I will. And maybe that's what my life is all about."

Cael nodded, calmly and confidently. I found his reaction odd. Again, I got the impression that this was some kind of quiz, and he was the self-appointed game leader.

*

"I see we're back to me," I mumbled. "Cael, I'm beginning to think you're as secretive about yourself as I had to be when I was a restaurant critic."

"Not at all," he assured me, even shaking his head slightly. "You just have to ask the right questions." Then he smiled, of course, but in a most friendly way.

I suddenly remembered a session I had with some friends and an Ouija board, when I was in my teens. I was involved in lots of stuff of that nature, growing up.

We were sitting in a circle on the floor, with the Ouija board in the middle. It was late at night, of course. We giggled a lot. It was tantalizing in a way not too different from a flirt with the hope of leading to seduction.

After some rounds of semi-serious questions, I needed to challenge both me and the board. So, I asked the age-old existential question, "Why am I here?"

I was whispering so low, little more than just thinking it. My friends could not hear me. They put their index fingers on the planchette and it immediately started moving on the board with the alphabet in capital letters.

It started slowly, moving here and there on the board. Suddenly it stopped over the letter M. After a short pause, it continued to O and then M. Then it went back to its original position. It had spelled MOM.

Well, duh...

I am here because of my mom. Sure, that is true for any person, but in my case even more so. My mother had set her mind on reproducing with the man who became my father. She explained to me that he had perfect teeth. But that isn't how genetics work. I have not.

We made a round, and when it was again my turn I had to give it another try. I asked, "Who am I?" The planchette first landed on S, and I thought it was going to spell Stefan. It would be true, of course, but a bummer. Then it quickly moved through A – T – A – N.

I quit my existential questions after that.

I was pulled out of my memories by that xylophone laughter I had gotten to know quite well. Cael looked at me with a grin of great amusement.

"What?" I asked.

"You tell me," he said.

I fell back into my thoughts. I have tried several occult methods – mostly, but far from only, in my young years. Hypnosis, the I Ching, the Tarot, astrology, palmistry, you name it. They could really impress me at times. I mean really.

But I found them all consistent on one and the same point. If I tried a question relating to the purpose of my life or the meaning of it all, they would just reply with balderdash. If I insisted, they would get threatening, as if angrily disapproving. Like the Ouija board.

Some things about life you just have to figure out on your own.

"Ain't that the truth!" Cael concluded, seemingly out of nowhere.

"What is?"

"What you said. Suddenly one day you will connect the dots, and that's what your life is all about."

"Aha," I said, still feeling a bit confused. "I certainly hope so. Otherwise, I will not die without moaning."

I tried a laugh, but it didn't work out that well. It sounded like I coughed.

*

I leaned forward over the table, catching Cael's eyes and sticking to them. He had no problem with that. It was more distracting to me, since up close his countenance was even more striking. One could easily get lost in it.

I blinked to snap out.

"Now it's your turn, Cael. You must tell me what you might have found out about the meaning of it all."

"There's still plenty of time for that," he replied. "I promise."

I glanced at the big clock by the buffet. It was about a quarter to twelve. Only forty-five minutes had passed since we began our brunch. I could have sworn it was longer.

"Please, you have to give me something. Otherwise I'll start feeling like a lab rat."

He laughed and put his hand on mine, which was resting on the table. His skin was still dry and rather cool, as if we were outdoors. The fingers were exceptionally slim and long. A pianist's dream. The nails were immaculate. Maybe he was a model, and that was how he made his money. He should be.

"I'll tell you this for now," he said. "I make the meaning."

"You make your meaning of life? You don't search for it, but decide what you want it to be?"

He nodded.

"That too. It's the same."

I thought about it for a moment.

"That could work, I guess." After thinking of it some more, I added, "Maybe that's really what we all do."

"Yes."

Tao

Cael lifted his hand from mine and grabbed his glass. I felt a wave of disappointment through my body. I hoped it didn't show on my face. When he had sipped some Champagne, he continued.

"We'll get back to that, don't you worry. But now I want us to dwell on that thing about Do and Tao. You said their meanings differ."

"You've read the book, so you must have some idea."

"You wrote it."

I had to give him that. Also, I didn't mind at all expanding on this subject.

"It's obvious to me that Lao Tzu understood Tao as what we today call a law of nature," I started, sounding a bit too much like holding a lecture. "*The* law of nature," I added, "by which all of the cosmos and everything in it is ruled. Sort of a unified field theory."

"That sounds quite modern for a text more than two thousand years old."

"I know. There's a risk of anachronism. One should be wary of getting blinded by how we look at things today. But I can't see a better explanation for it. All through the Tao Te Ching, what he describes about Tao keeps coming back to it as a law of nature. Lao Tzu was doing what so many did in antiquity – he tried to figure out how the world works. Since he could see that it displays patterns and regularities, it must be orderly, and any order has rules."

"Isn't that also what religions try to do – explain how the world works?"

"Indeed. But Lao Tzu has more in common with the Greek philosophers, who were his contemporaries although on the other side of the world. Like them, he had no need of gods in his cosmology. He regarded nature as its own majesty, ruled by a principle rather than a person."

"But didn't his Tao have personal traits?"

"Not really. Well, he did describe it with such words at times. What Tao prefers, and so on. But that can be said about a law, too. There is always intention behind a law, an objective at which it aims. It's just that this law is its own objective. Tao is not a law founded by another. It is both the end and the means, the architect and the builder in one."

"Wouldn't that be what is usually called a god?"

I flinched at his comment.

"You got me there."

I rewarded him with a smile, which was not as comfortable as I wanted it to be. But I had my objections.

"What we use the word god for is not at all something well defined. Mostly, it just applies to the god of the three monotheistic religions – Judaism, Christianity and Islam. They have set the standard for what we call god, as well as what we call religion. But these definitions don't fit the other beliefs. They don't have gods in the same way. They're not even religions in the same way. Their deities, or whatever to call them, are not alone, nor are they alone as architects of the world. Many of them had nothing to do with its formation, according to the creation myths. Usually they are little more than inhabitants of the world, although different from humans. Superior to us, but still far from perfect or omnipotent."

"But couldn't Taoism be described as monotheism, with Tao being a god similar to Yahweh?"

"The Tao Te Ching mentions a deity only once. That's in chapter four, where it says that Tao seems to precede the ancestor of all. That ancestor is Ti, the first and supreme deity according to ancient Chinese mythology."

"There you go. Ti is their Yahweh."

I allowed myself a grin, since I knew I had this covered.

"But Lao Tzu thereby states that Tao is something else than Ti or any other deity. It precedes them. In other words, even a creator deity like Ti had to follow the laws of Tao. In the same chapter, Lao Tzu says that Tao seems to be the origin of all things. And he says that he doesn't know whose child it is, meaning nothing preceded it."

"Or he just doesn't know."

I let out a grunt. Cael was quick. Whatever views he nourished on the subject, I had a growing suspicion that he was mainly interested in teasing me. I could live with that, since it would increase the chances of another xylophone solo emanating from that charming smile of his. But I was yet far from defeated.

"That could be it," I admitted. "Still, as far as I can see, Lao Tzu regarded Tao as something we would call a law of nature, and not a deity of any kind. His Taoism was a consequence of his cosmology. The whole text of his repeats that one should understand and obey this law of nature, since anything else is doomed to fail. Tao is not a judge, condemning people to some kind of punishment for disobeying the law. It is just the way things are."

"A very different kind of god, then."

"Very different," I confirmed. "As a matter of fact, so different that it would be inadequate to call Tao a god at all. And certainly, Taoism cannot be called a religion."

I leaned back in my chair, rather pleased with myself, and had a sip of the Champagne. We had finished our plates, but were in no immediate hurry to refill them.

*

"Stop me if I get boring," I continued while looking at my Champagne glass as if it were a TV set, "but I've studied a number of mythologies, and a lot of them deal with trying to explain the world and phenomena in it. That's particularly true for creation myths. They are usually quite logical, especially if the culture where they were invented is taken into account. They try their best to explain how the world may have emerged at the dawn of time. That makes them cosmological theories of sorts, and some are strikingly clever."

"You haven't bored me yet," Cael assured me as I paused shortly.

"For example, there's the Egyptian myth of the primordial deity Chepre, who was all alone. How to create other deities without having a mate? He masturbated and let his seed into his mouth, then spitting out the deities. He impregnated himself. An odd story, but a clever way to solve the problem of how the very first one can multiply."

"Odd, indeed."

"I hope I didn't offend you."

"Not a chance," he assured me with a wide smile. "I find it interesting that he used his head in the process."

"Well, I think the ancient Egyptian idea was that he mixed his semen with his saliva. In the past, the bodily fluids were often regarded as containing certain powers."

"But he did it in his head."

"Sure," I said and shrugged my shoulders. "You can even say that he gave himself head. A flexible deity."

Cael played his xylophone shortly.

"So," he said after a moment of silence, "instead of being mythologies disguising as cosmologies, many mythologies are really cosmologies in disguise?"

"That's my impression."

"It makes sense. But why do you think so many of them have the creation process managed by persons instead of pure principles, to use your wording? That's far from only in the monotheistic myths."

"You're right. It's common. Deities aren't always there to begin with, but they always participate in the process of creation, and quite often there is indeed a deity commencing it."

"So, what does that tell you?"

Although his question was straightforward, it had some odd innuendo. I wondered what he was implying with it. Cael did not strike me as a religious fundamentalist – not at all. Still, his question indicated some kind of religious agenda. If so, I would probably soon learn of it.

A renewed curiosity about this young man rose in me. I was not to give up turning the topic of our conversation from me to him, but that would have to wait just a little longer. First, I had to answer his question in my way, however he might react to it.

"I think ancient minds needed the idea of a will behind what happened, especially something that grand. Like Aristotle's idea about a first mover. When something is moved there has to be someone moving it. An intention. It was very hard for our ancestors to imagine something happening by itself, automatically. So, they thought of deities. These deities were anthropomorphic – kind of human but both older and grander, or their feats could not have preceded and exceeded those of humans. People tried to explain the world in a way that they could themselves understand."

Cael looked away, in the direction of the buffet. It was the first time his eyes were elsewhere when he addressed me.

"What if they were right?"

*

I stared at him until his eyes returned to me. It didn't take that long.

"Cael, are you a religious man?"

He burst into a laughter that was louder and longer than any of the previous ones. The xylophone went into a crescendo.

I couldn't imagine what he found so terribly amusing with my question. It seemed from the laughter that his answer to the question must be no. But that didn't explain what he found so hysterical, especially considering his previous question, surprising me by hinting at a religious belief I would not have guessed he nourished.

Was it that he thought I was a religious man? Had I given him any reason to think so? Hardly. At least not religious in the sense shared by the three monotheisms.

I had to wait for his explanation. It took a while.

As his volcanic laughter went on, I checked around in the Peacock Alley. Nobody paid any attention to us, although Cael was so loud. They were probably determined to be discreet. The pianist kept playing and singing, unaffected by Cael's laughter although he must have heard it.

"I am so enjoying this conversation," Cael said when he had finally stopped laughing.

"Evidently," I mumbled. "Pray tell, what was so funny?"

"I can't explain. Maybe I was just so surprised to get that question."

"So, I guess you're not."

"Not what?"

"Religious."

"As in believing something I have no way of knowing? As in worshiping some superior being? Not at all." He struggled not to start laughing again. "It's just about the furthest thing from my mind."

"Good for you," I said, still rather baffled by his amusement, which seemed to keep on sort of bubbling inside of him.

"Now you," Cael said. "I asked you a question you only answered with another question."

"What if they were right, you mean?"

He nodded. He concentrated on me, his wild amusement replaced with curiosity.

"But," I had to object, "I thought we just established that you don't believe in that stuff at all."

"Not exactly. Anyway, what would be your reply?"

What now? Was he contradicting what he had just said? Was he religious in some way, after all?

It hit me that he might be a Buddhist. In my experience, they can be anywhere between devout believers and crass materialists. A lot of Buddhism is void of gods as such. Zen most definitely is. Still, they can have some concepts that come close to the divine. Whatever the case with Cael, I felt obliged to answer his question the best I could.

"I guess you mean, what if they were right about the universe having to be created by a will of some kind, as opposed to just appearing pretty much out of nowhere, like the Big Bang theory has it?"

He nodded, and his face expressed increasing curiosity. He really wanted to know.

"In short, I don't find it impossible. How plausible it is, I have no idea. But I do think we are still very far from understanding how the universe appeared, or if it has always existed – in one or other form."

"Go on," he urged me when I closed my mouth. He was obviously convinced that I had more to say on the subject.

He was not wrong.

"Already the Greek philosophers were aware of the problem with something out of nothing. It just can't be. A Big Bang out of nothing defies the logic that the universe seems to contain. And if it's out of something, then there is another truer emergence to be found, preceding the Big Bang. Or there is something that has always existed, out of which our universe was born. I think the multiverse theory is a way of trying to solve that paradox. It suggests that universes give birth to other universes in an endless chain. In any case, Big Bang is not the final answer."

I had to take a sip of Champagne. It felt quite fitting. Cael joined me, but was in more of a hurry to put the glass back on the table than I was. So, I continued.

"But the paradox isn't solved with a creator. Then we have to ask where he came from. However we tackle the problem, we're back to something out of nothing. As one of the Greeks said, I don't remember who – either the world has always existed or it never did. The former seems to be the most likely."

I allowed myself a smile. Cael just nodded. Evidently, we didn't have the same sense of humor.

"And the creator?" he asked.

"In an eternal universe, there is no need for one. But there could be one. There could be an eternal creator making temporary universes. If they have a maker, they must be regarded as temporary, because then they have a starting point. Probably also an ending point."

"Only things with a beginning have an end," Cael added.

"Precisely."

"Most things haven't."

"That, I wouldn't know."

*

We decided that it was time to make a new excursion to the buffet, this time for meat dishes.

"Contrary to much of the seafood," I said, "meat needs skillful preparations. It's more of a challenge for the chef. Well, already Lao Tzu said that cooking a small fish is a delicate matter, but it will do without almost any elaborate cooking. With meat dishes you usually have to do a lot more to make them tasty and pleasant to consume. We'll see what this kitchen can muster."

"Should we order red wine?" Cael inquired.

"First, let's see how the Champagne manages. Good Champagne can do surprisingly well also with meat dishes. And we still haven't finished the bottle."

Cael had no objection. We got new plates and took a tour around the tables laden with all kinds of meat, before picking anything.

"About that creator," I said as we were doing our reconnaissance, "I think we would need to leave our anthropomorphic prejudice. It doesn't have to be a personal being along the line of humans, or for that matter any other animals. The bible says that God created humans in his image, but it's more likely that we created him in ours. If there is such a thing as a creator of some sort, we can't expect it to be like us in any way."

"Can't it be?"

"It can, I guess, but it seems so far-fetched – or should I say near-fetched? It would be like a parody, and not very divine at all."

I could see that Cael was about to burst into one of his laughs, but he restrained himself. Bits of it escaped his nose instead, almost like sneezing.

"An eternal creator would need to be impersonal," I

continued, "because eternity is a lonely place where nothing can make a difference. If the creator is the only thing eternal, he would be sort of invisible to himself, since he has always been and always will be. That's status quo. Stillness. Like the Talking Heads sing, 'A place where nothing ever happens.' Eternity must be something as close to nothing as ever possible. So, it would be much more similar to Lao Tzu's Tao than to any deity. That is to say, it would be little else than a law of nature, out of which universes are born. So, we're back to an impersonal creation."

"You're saying the creator can't be aware of himself?"

"Not without having something to compare himself with. He'd just be a constant presence, sort of like someone living his whole life in a dark room without sound, even without walls, floor and ceiling. A void. Coming to think of it, he would be nothing but a void."

"That doesn't sound like much fun," Cael said, again with an expression of withholding a laugh. "Couldn't he at least think? Or dream?"

"About what? No, only if he happened to create a world that he was able to observe, would he be aware of himself – as something separate from that world."

"Then he would have to create the world, wouldn't he? To become aware of himself."

"There are creation myths suggesting something like that. Even Genesis of the bible, where God seems to create the world and its inhabitants to have something to relate to. Before creation, he just hovers over the dark abyss of the primordial sea. That's an image of empty space, I'd say. And a famous hymn of the Rig Veda states that the primordial one was enclosed in nothing, but emerged by a heat that is described as desire. The desire to end the desolation."

I had a great time. These kinds of topics always got me going.

The Art of Chateau Latour

As we were talking – well, mostly me – we picked some samples here and there from the many meat dishes. It was rather random and our choices were similar but not identical.

Mainly, I took less of each thing than Cael did. As the food on his plate piled up I wondered if he would be able to eat it all.

I had to try a slice of crispy Canadian bacon and some honey glazed steamship ham, both very appealing to the eyes as well as the nose. Then I carefully picked a couple of the most intriguing sausages and some roast leg of lamb. I added a slice of Beef Wellington and a few spoonfuls of the dark gravy they had prepared to accompany it.

After some salad for the remaining space on the plate, I was ready to return to our table. Soon, so was Cael.

When we sat down, Cael hurried to pour up the last of the Champagne and raise his glass.

"To the end of desolation!" he said with a most joyous smile.

We toasted and emptied the glasses. As I was looking at my plate, contemplating with what to start, Cael spoke again.

"If I understand you correctly, there can't really be a beginning of the universe, and there can't be a conscious creator of it. I'm starting to wonder, do you think there can be a universe at all?"

I chuckled. I do take delight in questions that approach the absurd.

"Probably not."

"So where are we?"

"In the idea of one?" I suggested, keeping my smile on. "Schiller said that the universe is one of God's thoughts. I like that he said 'one of.' Let's not take for granted that we are the main characters of the play."

"Didn't you just say that God can't have any thoughts?"

"I know. But I like the idea of comparing the Big Bang theory to getting an idea. It pops up, seemingly out of nowhere, and then it blooms and blooms. Like the 'Fiat!' of Genesis. Let there be this, let there be that. That's how ideas are, and society is created and recreated by them."

*

Our waiter arrived with a bottle of red wine and two proud Bordeaux glasses. Cael must have ordered it at the buffet, when I didn't notice. And not just any bottle. It was the famous Pauillac wine Chateau Latour, Premier Cru, from 1998. Not the best year for Bordeaux reds – but hey!

I didn't know the price, but I had no doubt it was beyond what I could afford.

"It's on me," Cael hurried to say.

I would still have worried tremendously, if it were not for the waiter nodding as Cael said so. He confirmed it, which was a bit odd, but it made me relax.

"I don't know how to thank you," I said. "This is something I wouldn't dream of allowing myself, especially not in a restaurant."

I've had my share of fine wines, usually when I didn't have to pay for them. The best ones are out of this world. Really. Your pallet marvels at a beverage with such complexity and balance. It is unreal, like a drink from the gods.

"Well, we've been talking about the divine for so long," Cael said. "It's time we drink it, too."

"Yes, that should be it," I said, and my voice was sort of floating away into a daydream.

The waiter rewarded our appreciation with a pleased smile, as he pulled out the cork and let us inspect it. Nothing to worry about. He poured a little into each glass, and waited patiently for our judgment.

We did the whole thing, leaning the glasses to look at the color against the white table cloth, spun them around a little to release the bouquet and inhaled it, took a sip and let it roll on the tongue while we sucked in air between slightly parted lips. Then we swallowed, to feel the beverage make its way through the gullet.

The wine had not yet opened. That would take some more contact with the air. But it was already evident that this wine was a wonderful treat. We nodded happily to the waiter, who refilled our glasses.

When he was gone, I had to tell Cael, as I was staring at the bottle standing majestically in the middle of the table:

"You must make a bundle of money to afford this."

"I manage," he said casually.

"Obviously you do. Can I ask if you're a model? You certainly have the looks for it."

"Well, I'd like to see myself as a role-model," he said jokingly. "But that's it. I simply make my money."

"Make them, like a counterfeiter?"

There was the xylophone laughter again.

"No, it's as real as can be. All I make is real."

It was obvious I had to settle with that, although it was not very informative. However he made his money, he was not inclined to tell me about it. Fine.

My fantasy went wild.

*

We toasted without words and drank some wine with what must be described as piety.

"Now that we indulge in the nectar of the gods," Cael said, still holding the glass up, "why don't we continue on that very subject?"

"For an atheist, you're quite interested in deities."

"Atheist? I wouldn't put it exactly like that."

"So, how would you put it?"

"Maybe like Hamlet. You know the quote, 'There are more things in heaven and earth, Horatio, than are dreamt of in your philosophy.' Deities are just names, and the name that can be named..."

I nodded with pleasure at his short quotes from Shakespeare as well as the Tao Te Ching. Two splendid sources for a conversation. I still had to reflect on how he used them.

"As for dreams," he continued, "well, they are more than mere dreams. So, I'm not inclined to state what is not. The mere denial of something makes it real in some way, or it wouldn't be there to be denied. Everything exists, in one way or other. Even deities. In one way or other."

"But didn't you say earlier that you don't believe in them?"

"No. I said I don't believe in something I have no way of knowing, and I don't worship a superior being."

"Isn't that the same?"

"No." He smiled teasingly. "Now, let's try the wine with our food, shall we?"

"Cael, it's not easy to make sense of what you say," I complained and shook my head. But I was still amused by how he intrigued me.

*

I excluded the bacon immediately. It wouldn't stand a chance against this wine. Their meeting would just be awkward. I considered the ham and sausages shortly, and the leg of lamb for a little while. But then I decided to go directly to the Beef Wellington. Nothing else would be more of a challenge for the Latour.

Not even the beef was, I found out when trying it. There was nothing wrong with this Wellington. Its interior was dramatically red, its coating was thick with flavor from the goose liver and duxelles, and its puff pastry wrap was crisp and fluffy. But still, the Latour in all its splendor just owned it and shadowed it.

No kitchen trickery could match such a wine. That would take the very best of ingredients, cooked exactly to the point of their own perfection. For tenderloin, that meant it had to be blue, as the French call it, which is practically raw. Anything else and this wine would just drown the meat, almost with contempt. It showed the Wellington some mercy for trying so hard, but no noticeable respect.

I thought that the only thing on the buffet worthy such wine was the paddlefish caviar, although that would be far from a match made in heaven. Slices of the famous Pata Negra ham might work better, but I couldn't remember having seen it on the buffet. The steamship ham I had on my plate didn't manage that well. A sip of wine made it go away, like a faded memory of the past.

The leg of lamb fared better, of course. At least, it was saying to my taste buds that red wine was the thing. But this particular wine was quick to overwhelm the meat and scare it into hiding in my stomach.

The wine was gentle like a caress can be in a dream, never in reality. Its harmony was impeccable, with nothing sticking out of the composition as a whole.

This was a wine to inspire poets and at the same time

make them gladly forget their vocabulary.

I wondered if the wine could have an interesting dialogue with proud Kalamata olives, and considered searching the buffet for them. And game, for sure! Did they have any deer or moose, perchance? That would do it, if properly treated.

"Not bad, is it?" Cael said, refilling our glasses.

"We will feel this superb aftertaste a week from now. It's things like this that make me have faith in mankind, after all."

"What more?"

"Art. Leonardo da Vinci, Picasso, Beethoven, Shakespeare, Dostoyevsky, Fellini, Nijinsky, Edith Piaf, and so on. Ars longa, vita brevis."

"They're all dead. Where's the hope in that?"

"New ones appear. Not frequently, but they do pop up now and then. And a Leonardo is worth waiting for."

"No argument there," Cael said and took another sip from his glass, almost purring from delight. Then he focused on me again. "What *is* art?" he asked.

"Creativity," I replied immediately.

"Which is...?"

"The joyous extraction of something new out of the old."

"Not out of nothing, I gather," Cael commented with a smile. "You're not fond of nothing, we've already established."

"It can't be done. Plato had the idea of primordial forms existing in sort of a dimension of ideas, hidden inside the reality we perceive. Also to him, something out of nothing was inconceivable. A seed could become a plant, because the final form was already somewhere. We call it genetics."

"But what does genetics have to do with art? Not even

the children of the artists you mentioned inherited their genius."

"You can say that again," I replied with a grunt. "It's usually an embarrassing fiasco when they try. That's why nepotism is so detrimental to society."

"As for art, then?"

"I refer to how ideas multiply. The artist gets an idea and builds on it. The idea is the seed. The finished piece of art is the plant. What leads it to its completion is an innovative way of combining what already exists. Look at the Stone Age cave paintings in Lascaux and Altamira, which are more than fifteen thousand years old. Others are twice that age. They all depict animals and other things well known to the artists."

"But artists have made non-existent creatures, as well."

"When mythological beasts were invented, they were combinations of known animals, and not complete figments of the imagination. Dragons were lizards with bird wings. The griffin combined the lion and the eagle. The centaur was a man glued to a horse. And so on."

"You're saying it would be impossible to create something, without the use of what's already there?"

"Yes. As much as I adore our ability to fantasize, I'd say we go blank if we don't have anything on which to build our fantasies. There is no creation out of nothing. Look at dreams, where the mind can go wild. But they're always made up of experiences, no matter how absurd they are."

"So, artist are little more than plagiarists of sorts?"

"Still, creative fantasy can come up with things that were never before imagined. That's its forte, and the source to art. Out of known things, something completely new can be constructed. And creativity can reach a new understanding of old phenomena – that's science."

"So, science is an art?"

"Or art is science. That's pretty much what Leonardo da Vinci suggested in his notes, although he didn't state it with those exact words. His approach to art was what we would call scientific, and his way of doing science was quite artistic. Artists and scientists both relate to their subjects as things of beauty."

"Ah, beauty. We've touched on that before."

"Have we?" I wondered.

I was not sure. Certainly, the concept is something I regard as very significant in the human nature, and the face before me was an impressive example. But had we talked about it?

"Maybe just indirectly," Cael suggested.

"When I was an adolescent, I decided that beauty is the closest thing we have to evidence of something divine."

"Divine, you say?" Cael inquired with a scoundrel kind of smile.

I nodded, returning it.

"Yes, imagine that. But the divine within us all, not outside of us. Our perception of beauty suggests it. It's something else than what can be explained by Darwinism and biology in general. We find beauty in things that have nothing to do with our survival and reproduction. Actually, we prefer it in things that have absolutely no functional use. Art for art's sake. I don't say it's proof of the existence of a god, but of something other than the material world of cause and effect, survival of the fittest, and so on. Beauty at least suggests there is something more, something sort of sacred that we are connected to, or carry within us."

"The magic of it all?"

I shrugged my shoulders.

"Something like that," I replied and had a sip of wine. Its gentle caress distracted me for a moment. "Dostoyevsky said that beauty will save the world. It was in The Idiot, of course. You know what they say – children and fools tell the truth. For the rest of us, it's more complicated to know it as well as tell it."

"The truth," Cael said, tasting the word as if it were another sip of the wine. "What is truth?"

I had to laugh.

"I quote Dostoyevsky, and you reply with a quote of Pontius Pilate."

"Or Bulgakov."

"Yes, I love his somber version of the meeting between Jesus and Pilate, in The Master and Margarita. Indeed, what is truth? And who can claim to own it? I can't speak for Dostoyevsky, but as I see it, beauty is the only thing that can save the world, because without it there is no incentive to save anything at all. It's very simple. We won't save the world unless we want to, and beauty awakens that want."

"Wouldn't that be love?"

I let out a grunt.

"You're a persistent one, aren't you?"

He replied with a grin.

"I guess you could say that," I admitted. "It depends on how you define love."

"As in caring tremendously for something. As in reacting to someone or something with a sense of euphoria."

"In that case, yes."

"I told you, Stefan. Don't give up on love just yet."

"I'll admit to being a lover of the arts."

Sweet Loneliness

We turned our attention to our plates and the wine, for a while. I checked that big clock in the middle of the lobby, surrounded by the buffet tables. It was five past twelve. Only twenty minutes had passed since last I checked. I would have guessed the double.

Perhaps I didn't remember correctly what time it had been last? But I knew I arrived at eleven. Had I just spent a little more than an hour at the Waldorf Astoria?

Maybe it was just that I was getting a bit drunk from the wine we consumed.

Usually, time passes this slowly only when I am really bored. But I wasn't. Although we mainly talked about me – honestly, I did most of the talking, too – I was enjoying Cael's company. Not only because of his spectacular looks. He was delightful company, and what little he said was worth listening to, far from only because it was mostly about me.

Being the subject of the conversation was not what I was used to. And this was practically an interview, so far. Most often, I manage to have it the other way around. But this Cael, he beat me at my own game. So far. We would get to him. He had promised it, and there was still plenty of time.

Nonetheless, I thought I should move things ahead by asking about him. But Cael was quicker.

"So, you're a lover of the arts, Stefan. What about people?" he asked just as I opened my mouth. "You have no love for them?"

"That's much more complicated than with art. They interfere with whatever emotions they evoke in me. Art gently allows itself to be loved, without objections. With people it's another thing. They react, and every so often they tend to disappoint."

I thought about something from the *Peanuts* comic strip. Linus wants to be a doctor when he grows up, but his sister Lucy objects that he can't, because he doesn't love mankind. Linus protest, "I love mankind! It's people I can't stand." I could relate to that.

"You love mankind?" Cael asked, surprising me by happening to get so close to what was on my mind.

"Sure I do," I said, probably not sounding that very convincing. "At least I *like* mankind. Most people, too, but rarely enough to stand their company at length. I get bored. Then I get irritated, and leave before getting insulting or even aggressive. I am easily bored."

*

Although I said it as if this was something I had always known about myself, that was not the case. I didn't realize it until I was told, which was by a fascinating woman I met on my second visit to the United States, when this millennium was new. That trip took me to Los Angeles.

Charlotte Zutrauen was in her nineties, and I wouldn't hesitate to call her a guru. A lot of Hollywood big shots held her in the same high esteem, and consulted her about matters that were important to them. She was fascinating, indeed. The word doesn't even begin to do her justice.

A friend and I picked her up in her house, high up on the Hollywood Hills. It was quite a scary ride on the narrow road, spiraling up the steep hill. We were going to have lunch downtown.

Charlotte was as skinny as she was energetic, vibrant of life. She treated me like we had been friends forever. Already on the way down that steep hill, mere minutes after we met for the first time, she said quite bluntly to me that I got bored with everything and everyone after a while, and I should not feel guilty about it.

It may sound simple enough, but to me it was a revelation. Suddenly, I could fit a lot of pieces in my mind as well as in my past together. It made me even dizzier than the scary car ride down that narrow road.

When I was back in Sweden, I told my mother about this encounter and what the old woman had said about me. She listened attentively, and then she just nodded with a short grunt.

We never talked about it before – or since – but she immediately confirmed, as if having known it all the time. Either that or she realized when hearing it, as I had done.

*

"Oh, I hope you don't find me boring," Cael said with a smile that revealed he had no such fear.

"Not yet," I dared to reply and returned his smile. "Far from it. I look forward to finally learning more about you."

"Isn't there anyone who never bores you?"

"Me. I'm never bored by me, what pops up from inside my head and what thoughts I get from looking at the world around me."

"Of course," Cael said, but in a soothing rather than teasing way.

"That's what stands in the way of me taking time with others. I'm fine for a few hours, but then I come to realize that I prefer my own company and they get in the way."

"So, you're not the marrying kind."

"Really not. My relations have been few and short, none leading to that kind of commitment."

I paused briefly, overcome by a cavalcade of memory fragments. Some of them had a certain sting.

"I guess I learned it from my mother," I resumed, after putting a stop to the sudden rush of memories. "She tried marriage for a few years, and then never again. One could even say she never really tried it. I was a little kid at the time – part of the bargain, as they say. She told her husband to be that I was her child, not his, so she would pay my costs – and he should not interfere with how I was raised."

Cael's xylophone played a short arpeggio.

"Indeed, that's not what marriage is supposed to be about," he commented.

"Since she had already tried it, I never felt the need to do so. Even a shared household, outside of wedlock, I've only had very briefly. It didn't attract me much. I quickly got increasingly impatient with my partner. I'm no fun to live with, no fun at all. It's just not my thing. I'm in desperate need of my own space, and a lot of it."

"Don't you ever feel lonely?"

"All the time. But I don't find it agonizing. Not at all. To me, loneliness is pretty close to bliss."

There was a moment of silence. I had to look away from Cael's penetrating eyes.

"I know it sounds terrible, but what can I do?"

"I assure you I can relate to it," Cael said, again with a soothing voice, which did comfort me quite a bit. "I'm eternally fascinated by what comes out of my mind. But it doesn't contradict what happens around me. It's all the same."

"Well, we all perceive the outer world with our minds, so in a way it's kinds of the same."

"That, too," he agreed, shrugging his shoulders.

I didn't understand his remark. In what other way could it possibly be the same?

"The Swedish writer Hjalmar Söderberg wrote that he believed in the lust of the flesh and the incurable loneliness of the soul. I guess you wouldn't subscribe to that?"

"I couldn't, since it would be wrong."

"Morally wrong, you mean? If you pardon my saying so, you don't strike me as very virtuous."

"The soul can't be lonely. Then it wouldn't be a soul."

"That, you have to explain." I was bothered by the uncompromising way he put it. "As for me, I don't really understand the concept of the soul. I'm not even sure how to tell it apart from what we call the spirit."

"The soul is exactly our sense of belonging. All living creature have it. Otherwise they couldn't be alive."

"So, it's a life force?"

"No, that would be the spirit. The soul is the connection to it all, what makes you feel part of it as well as able to tell you apart from everything else in it."

"Isn't that our consciousness?"

"That's what makes us reflect on it, but we could not do that without feeling it. Much like something can't come out of nothing."

"Are you sure that the soul, the spirit and our conscious thought are not really one and the same?"

"Everything is one and the same. The universe is simple that way. Of course, when I describe the soul, the spirit and consciousness, I'm talking about aspects, not essence."

"Of course," I repeated with a grin. "Silly me."

"Your soul can tell you that," he told me with just as wide a grin.

At the same time as I was trying to come up with something ironic to say, I realized that I could in fact relate to the sensation he suggested. The feeling of oneness. I had always felt it, already as a little child. In those days it was even stronger, maybe simply because I didn't have too much else to think about.

Walking city streets at night, patting a purring cat, riding a subway packed with commuters, taking a deep breath surrounded by trees in a park, or at the beach dipping my naked foot into the water to check its temperature. I could feel it anywhere and anytime, the sense of belonging that Cael called the soul.

The feeling was undeniable, and I was not ignorant of its significance. It meant something. The curiosity of what that could be, I had carried with me since early childhood.

I was surprised to realize that my eyes had moistened. I blinked hard to snap out of it and stop the tears from coming. I looked up at Cael. His grin had receded to a kind and caring smile.

"I told you," he said.

Was I that easy to read? Had he sensed that I shared his conviction? It worried me, but at the same time it was a pleasant sensation, like getting naked in front of another person and finding that it was just fine. The consolation of sharing.

Well, I was still pretty much the only one getting naked – although, in all fairness, Cael in his youthful beauty was really the one who should be. The thought brought my face back to a smile. I hoped that he didn't figure out why. I saw no sign of it on his face.

*

"Beauty and love have one thing in common," I said, bringing it up partly in an effort to distract him from somehow concluding what beauty my mind had considered, just now.

"They make people possessive. They want to hang on to it, chain it and keep it to themselves. If they succeed, they are bound to kill it."

"People are desperate," Cael commented with a blank expression on his face.

"True. We know that nothing lasts, but still we struggle to keep things as they are, forever. Well, the things we like. But the nature of beauty is evanescent. It comes and it goes, like the headlight of a passing car at night. That's what makes it so exquisite. If we were able to grab hold of it, we would get used to it and soon enough the beauty would fade. It would become ordinary. It's the same with love."

"Some say that love enhances beauty."

"It does, while it lasts. Indeed. I've seen it with my own eyes. Those I have loved became ever more wonderful to behold, as long as I did so."

"So, you have loved?"

"I confess that I have," I admitted, adding a brief smile. "That potent cocktail of lust, longing and possessiveness – I've drank it. Sometimes just a sip in passing, sometimes emptying the glass. It sure can make us do the most foolish things, and still adore every minute of it. But what a hangover! Love should be treated like beauty – with utmost care. But that takes an amount of discipline we rarely muster."

Cael took a sip from his glass and gently put it back on the table, before speaking.

"There's not much fun in discipline."

"Indeed not," I confirmed. "Failing can be a wonderful experience. It's when we think we can't fail that we head for catastrophe. And don't we make that mistake over and over!"

"But if failing is wonderful, is there really such a thing as failure?"

"Not every failure is wonderful. Some of them are dreadful."

My ears sort of buzzed, and I realized that the pianist had started one of my favorite songs – Bobbie Gentry's *Ode to Billie Joe* from the 1960's. What good timing! This bittersweet ballad is all about the untrustworthy nature of love.

A farmer family is having dinner when the news is passed with the biscuits on the dinner table:

Billy Joe MacAllister
Jumped off the Tallahatchie Bridge.

The lyrics slowly and vaguely reveal that the daughter of the family was his lover.

Although the Waldorf Astoria pianist's version was far from reaching the deep blue melancholia of Bobbie Gentry's original, I could feel tears forming in my eyes.

I'm hopelessly sentimental, and it has only gotten worse through the years.

"The best songs get you," I said, mostly talking to myself, "even when sung by far from the best artists. This one makes the mistake of performing instead of letting himself be seduced by the song. He uses the music to try to catch the audience. He should trust that the song itself can attract us, when sung from his own appreciation of it. In spite of his shortcomings, this song is able to reach out."

I glanced at Cael and could see that he was also listening to it. He turned to me.

"You speak about music the way you've spoken about food."

"Well, I was a music critic before starting to write about restaurants. I guess I used the same approach there."

"You've been a critic of both music and restaurants? Aren't you the lucky one."

"It was at separate times and for different newspapers. Music came first, when I lived in Stockholm. Mainly rock and pop. And like with food, far from every performance was a delight. Mostly we covered one hit wonders and such. Mainstream pop, produced in the factories of the major record labels. It was before the Internet, so there was not much else we could do than go with the flow of the music industry, where true talent is rare."

"Still, wouldn't that be the dream job for every young aspiring journalist? And wouldn't restaurant critique be the dream of journalists getting a little older?"

"Maybe so," I replied and shrugged my shoulders. "Dreams and reality don't always match that well."

I didn't bother to explain it to Cael, but it was my authorship that led me to those journalistic missions. It's common for authors to make their money on journalism. Few books sell enough to pay decently for the time spent writing them.

I had started, soon after my first book was released, writing literary reviews for a Stockholm newspaper. That is quite common among writers of fiction and poetry. It felt too close to home, so I was happy to move on to music, and then restaurants.

Being a critic is quite different from writing reports and news texts. It takes somebody with a language suitable to describe the arts and the emotional experience they give, as well as the integrity and sensitivity to judge to what extent they give it. Reporters are rarely adequately equipped for it. They tend to settle for calling things good or bad, and rating them in some numeric scale, as if art is just another sport with winners and losers, records and failures.

Poets are probably the best, because their language is the most sensitive and precise – if they are good poets, that is.

As a novelist, I guess my forte was to make the readers share the experience of a concert or a meal, and to describe the event so that it made some sense. Basically, I did what we all tend to do when exposed to art. I allowed it to influence me and then took note of what it made me think.

I knew I was good at it. Even excellent. But I was not about to tell Cael. I would only disgust myself if I did. The old Jante law...

We returned our attention to the song, listening in silence until the last lines, which finished on a darkly low note:

And me, I spend a lot of time
Pickin' flowers up on Choctaw Ridge,
And drop them into the muddy water
Off the Tallahatchie Bridge.

"The beauty of it," I said, needing to blink a few times to interrupt and hide my tears, "is that her grief, in all its torment, has brought meaning to her life. She would not have wanted to be without what caused it. The rain on her parade made it shine."

"People love to have loved."

"Exactly. Love of the past often surpasses it in the present."

"So, how about the love of the future?"

"The longing," I said with a bit of a sigh. "That's torture. We spend far too much energy dreaming about what might be. And what we wish for is usually not that pleasant when we happen to get it. The future rightly remains right there, forever tomorrow."

*

Cael put his elbow on the table to rest his head on his hand. The other hand was fiddling with his wine glass.

"For someone denying the existence of love," he said, "you're a hopeless romantic, Stefan."

"Hopeless, indeed," I replied.

"Do you sometimes wish it had turned out differently for you?"

"Never!" I answered so fast, he had barely completed the question. "You can't have the cake and eat it, too. It took me years to fully realize that, but since I did, I have come to terms with it. Well, sort of..."

I paused momentarily. My chest was contracting, making it hard to breathe. Something was gnawing inside of it, as if a parasite had entered and started its meal.

My voice darkened. The words were wrestling their way up my throat an out my mouth. I was not sure if Cael noticed.

"You make your life choices. Sometimes regretfully, but you would regret other choices even more. I have chosen. Of course, options may have been limited by conditions out of my control. But I've decided between the alternatives at hand, and I like to believe I got my priorities right. What else is there to do?"

I needed to have some wine, before continuing. The potent Latour was able to soothe me some.

"When I was young, I would sometimes think I was miserable, a failure of a human being, since I couldn't live like all the others seemed to do. And they seemed to enjoy it, too. But two things made me change my mind, ever so gradually. First, it dawned on me that those who got the things in life you're supposed to cherish, they weren't happy for very long. Their joy was temporary, mostly ending in at least the same amount of frustration, followed by disappointment. The boys who had the fortune of getting laid a lot in their teens, quickly found themselves married with children. The ball and chain. It was the same with the girls who could catch the number one jock in high school. Like Janis Ian sings in that wonderful ballad of hers, 'Love was meant for beauty queens and high school girls with clear skinned smiles, who married young and then retired.'"

"I've heard it," Cael said.

Talk about coincidences! The lobby pianist started playing a bossa nova rhythm, just like that of Janis Ian's song. And it was. He began to sing, "I learned the truth at seventeen..."

Had he heard us? No, that was not possible at this distance and with the noise from all the other people at the Peacock Alley.

It was painful. His version was no complete failure, although he was not able to sing it with the presence in the lyrics only accessible to the poet who wrote it, or a singer who had actually lived it. But I had already ventured into areas of my memory that still held the power to almost suffocate me. Again, I found it hard to breathe, before I was able to shake it off. A shiver went through me as I did.

"How about that," I said, throwing a glance at the pianist, but just because I needed to both speak and move in order to regain some kind of balance.

"The theme is not that different from the song we heard earlier. Stefan, you certainly are a hopeless romantic."

I didn't deny it. The songs were indeed similar in subject-matter. That would probably explain why the pianist played them both, and not that far apart.

"I saw them in my adolescence, those eager kids who greedily devoured all they could, as we the less fortunate witnessed in awe. We thought of them as Superman and Wonder Woman. But in mere years the price of that success was evident. They had blossomed in their teens and withered already in their twenties."

"Maybe they saw it differently."

I considered it shortly.

"Nah," I replied, and chuckled to make my response less hard. "I could see they didn't. In my envy, I really thought they would be happy ever after, but they soon proved otherwise."

I let out a sigh, as the faces of some friends from my adolescence passed before my inner eyes.

"I even formed a theory that I'm still inclined to support. Life gives you a certain quantity of success or blessings or what to call it. Almost like a bank deposit. Some fall for the temptation to spend it all in their teens. Maybe we all would if we could. Puberty has its fiery urges. Those who could, they were broke at twenty. The life remaining ahead of them was dull. They woke up from their party holiday, and it was Monday."

"Aren't you exaggerating?"

"Of course I was," I replied, consciously persisting with the past tense. "I was an adolescent. But I wasn't way off."

*

I raised my glass to have another sip of the wine and the solace it was able to bring. Cael swiftly raised his glass and did the same.

But the expression on his face showed that he had no need of the solace. He even looked quite jolly, almost to the point of making me feel insulted.

Without that charm of his, it would have hurt me. As it was, much to my surprise, his good mood actually comforted me – even more than the wine.

"And how about the other thing that made you change your mind?"

"Other thing? I forget."

"No you don't." He said it so firmly, were it not for the faint smile on his lips it would have been nothing less than a command.

"I guess it was time. I found I had a lot of it, because I didn't spend it on chasing that elusive happiness."

"Time?" Cael responded and then broke into his xylophone laughter. If it didn't sound so euphoric, I would indeed have been insulted. "You sweet fool! There is no time. There is all the time. Time is never an issue."

Choices

Although I felt more than a little bit provoked, his words were profoundly comforting. I couldn't understand why, but what he said made me feel relieved – right through to the very core of my being. As if my chest was torn open and an old shadow covering my body's interior finally fled, letting in the daylight.

A gasp escaped me. Though still completely mystified, I was suddenly lighter, almost to the point of levitating from the chair.

I had a feeling I knew why.

When I was twenty-five, getting my first book published, I was so impatient and full of energy to accelerate and take off. The world was to be my oyster, to borrow as we all do from Shakespeare.

But things slowed down, year by year. Obstacles and distractions multiplied, and my books took longer and longer to write. Life had so much else that stole my attention. Time became a rare commodity.

As the decades passed, I got increasingly displeased with my accomplishments. I wrote some books, and I like to think they were good ones. But I didn't write enough of them. Also, I lacked the additional time – or commitment – needed to properly care for them, once they were published.

I have always had a multitude of interests, and that's dangerous for an artist. You should do one thing, and do it all the time. I did not, and my career as a writer had suffered from it.

I accidentally confessed it to a friend, a bunch of years ago, when she asked what was my main gripe. I blurted out my answer in the form of a question, "Why am I not yet world famous?"

Silly me. Although I was just going through this in the privacy of my own mind, sitting in the Peacock Alley restaurant of the Waldorf Astoria, I could feel that I was blushing.

Of course, past time wasted is no obstacle to making better use of the future. When Cael boldly stated that time did not matter, that there would always be time, I snapped out of the many years of increased frustration. For the time being, at least. I had no idea how I would feel about it, once this Sunday brunch was over. Anyway, this moment of relief was a blessing, like a break for commercials in a horror movie on TV.

There was still time.

I blushed not only from the embarrassment of being so conceited, but also from the relief of still having time to make my grand ambition come true. And that in turn made me blush even more. My cheeks were burning. Cael didn't make any sign of noticing, or he just didn't care.

"So, what else do you have?" he asked.

*

"Else?" I repeated, still dizzy from the confusing relief I had just felt, mixed with the embarrassment my thoughts had given me.

"What was really your second reason for changing your mind?"

"But I just told you."

"That doesn't count," Cael said and waved it off. "Time is never an issue."

"So you said," I muttered, while I considered starting an argument about it.

But I could not deny that it had been a comforting. Also, without knowing exactly why, I was sure I would lose the argument. Then I remembered.

"Already as a little kid, I don't know what age, I tended to revolt against anything that was expected of me. And I don't mean homework, household chores and such – although I didn't do much of that, either. I mean how I was assumed to live my life."

"Now, we're getting somewhere," Cael commented briefly.

"I'm still like that. It feels like an instinct. I have a spontaneous reaction against anything that's expected of me. Social pressure. Conformity. Norms. I question them all and find it hard not to do the opposite, whenever that's possible. I think it's true for just about all my life choices. When one choice is obvious, I just have to go for another one. When opportunity knocks on the door, I tend to slam the door in its face. It's like I have this obsession to do the wrong thing."

"That must take its toll."

"Everything takes its toll. I told you, didn't I? Whatever choice you make in life, you have to pay for it. The question is what you get and how that compares to the cost. Some things are worth just about any cost."

"Have you chosen wisely, then?"

"I can only guess."

I had to pause to contemplate it. My mind quickly spun through a hoard of instances, where I had taken another path than the one that seemed obvious. Both in my private life and professionally.

Destroying relationships that could have been comforting, leaving places where I could very well have settled down, letting great opportunities slide away, quitting jobs that others would kill for, refusing to adapt even when it would have been a breeze, wasting away what could have become profitable resources.

Oh, I had done a lot of that. Like a grumpy child, sitting on the floor and yelling, "No, no, no!" Still, at just about every instant I had my reasons, even if they were mainly gut feelings.

"I think so," I concluded, although with audibly wavering conviction. "I just couldn't make myself behave any differently. It was always something from deep inside, overriding my conscious control."

"What was it?"

"I can only tell you what it felt like. And it may sound silly. It felt as if I had something else I must reach. Like destiny. Like I was meant for something particular, and anything else just had to go."

Cael sat very still, looking right at me as if looking right through me, at something happening way behind me. I was almost tempted to turn around and check.

"And what would that be?" he asked, somewhat like a teacher in class, testing a student's diligence with the homework.

I had to gather my thoughts. Not because I didn't know the answer, but I searched for the words to explain it properly. When I found them, I needed some additional time mustering the courage to utter them.

"The key to the true nature of the universe," I said, followed by a quick inhalation, as if bracing myself for a punch in the face.

Of course, I knew from my martial arts training that the best defense would be exhalation. So, that wasn't really it. My breath just had to do something.

Cael did nothing but wait for me to continue. So I did.

"Ever since childhood, I've felt that I am on an exploration. Some would call it a quest, but it feels much more like research. Gathering information, analyzing and coming to conclusions. I've done it through my writing, my painting, my aikido practice. Well, my whole life. Everything I've been up to is part of my exploration. And what I've tried to explore is the true nature of the universe, what this whole thing is all about."

I extended my arms to the sides in a big gesture, as an effort to visualize it. Immediately when doing so, I regretted it. The words needed no gesture, as Hamlet pointed out to the players. I let my arms fall to my sides.

"I have to confess that I settle for nothing less."

"The key to Tao?"

"The origin and true nature of Tao, yes. All that I've been doing with my life boils down to it. What is it, why is it, how is it?"

Cael nodded slowly. It was not a gesture of agreement, nor a sign that he prepared to object. It seemed like it was his way of merely confirming that he had registered my words.

"What makes you think you can get it?"

I blinked. Of course, there would be no way for me to claim something so preposterous. But Cael was not asking for proof of any kind. I was sure of that. He wanted to know what kept me going.

"I live in it. That means I must have access to it. It doesn't necessarily mean I will understand it, but it means I can. It is within our reach. All of us. It's even like the universe urges us to find it, teasing us by hinting that the answer is just around the corner. Frankly, I don't understand why everyone is not on the same exploration. Maybe they are."

"What have you found, so far?"

I sighed.

"What I have mostly found is what the universe is not. Mainly this: It's not at all what it seems to be."

"I say you've gotten quite far."

I glanced at Cael to check if he was ironic, but I saw no sign of it. He seemed to mean it sincerely.

"The next step is infinitely more difficult," I continued. "To go from what it isn't to what it truly is. I have this conviction, in my mind and in my body: The experiences I amass, the speculations I pursue, will one day lead me to the answer. To that, I devote my life. That's why I reject so much else, although it pains me to do so. Grieves me. But I feel I have no choice."

I halted as I felt estranged from that last remark. I needed to correct myself.

"It was the only choice worth making for a lifetime."

*

I was out of words. We looked at each other in silence for a while. I tried to read Cael's mind through his facial expression. It was neutral. The only thing emanating from it was its beauty. That satisfied me earlier in our conversation, but now it was not enough.

"Does it make any sense?" I asked, worrying about what his answer would be.

I even questioned myself. Was I just being naive, even delusional? A childish dreamer, refusing to accept reality? The hopeless romantic.

After quite some time in silent stillness, Cael nodded slowly.

"It makes perfect sense," he said with that very soft and gentle voice he had used a few times before. "It's the reason we are here."

About Time

Again, I was overwhelmed by that strange feeling of relief. This time it was even more tangible, like a straitjacket removed. Suddenly I was breathing much deeper. I had no idea what was happening to me, and I knew it would take some time to figure out why Cael's words had this effect.

"So, you also feel like your life has some kind of purpose that you need to find out?" I asked him when that sudden rush of relief had settled. It remained as a tickling sensation all over my body. It was sweet.

"Not really," he replied bluntly. "What I mean is that it's the reason you and I are here at the Waldorf Astoria Sunday brunch. Specifically."

I stared at Cael, not knowing what to ask in order for him to explain that strange statement.

"Enough with the roundabouts," he continued before I had a chance to figure something out. "Now it's my turn. I have prepared you enough."

"For what?" I wondered with a sense of imminent doom.

"Let's have some more food to accompany the rest of the wine, and to keep you in shape for the rest of our conversation."

I glanced at the bottle when he mentioned the wine, thinking that there couldn't be much left of it. But the bottle was three quarters full. Just as I was about to comment on it, Cael spoke again.

"What time is it?" he asked, looking right at me as if it was my job to keep track.

I glanced at the big lobby clock, but then my eyes remained there, staring. It was five past twelve, the same as it had been the last time I checked!

Sure, I'm lousy when it comes to keeping track of time as well as dates. Even years. And I had drunk some wine. But this was absurd. Cael just kept looking right at me. I opened my mouth, but he was quicker.

"Look again," he said.

I thought that was a good idea, since I was obviously mistaken. But when I looked anew, the clock was a quarter to twelve. Twenty minutes earlier than before! Immediately, I picked up my cell phone. It showed the same. A quarter to twelve. I almost dropped it, and hurried to put it back in my pocket.

"Time is relative," Cael said, keeping his eyes locked on mine.

I checked the lobby clock again. Still a quarter to twelve.

"What's going on?" I asked with but a whisper.

The pianist started playing another old favorite of mine, David Bowie's song *Time*. He sang the opening lines:

Time – he's waiting in the wings,
He speaks of senseless things,
His script is you and me, boy.

Cael's lips moved into a miniature smile, but he kept his eyes firmly on mine.

I turned my head to have a glance at the pianist, as if that would explain anything. Of course it didn't. He sat there, playing and singing, just like usual. But something else dawned on me. All the other tables in the Peacock Alley restaurant were empty. We were the only guests remaining, as far as I could see.

The staff was still there. I saw waiters walking around, whatever they might have to do now, and the cooks stayed at the buffet, taking good care of it. When did all the guests go, and how could I not have noticed?

Bewildered, I turned back to Cael, staring at him with wide eyes.

"I said it's about you and me, specifically." He paused a moment to let it sink in. Then he continued, "And the brunch, of course. So, should we have some more of it?"

He stood up and waited for me to do the same. After a while, I managed to do so, shivering and dizzy as if from a sudden blood pressure drop. I wondered if I would pass out.

"You won't," Cael said. "You have the imagination to handle this."

"I do?"

"You know you do."

Without understanding exactly what he expected me to handle, I agreed in my mind that my imagination had so far in life proven to jump effortlessly between absurdities. It was what it handled the best and enjoyed the most. I stopped shivering and my dizziness settled – well, partly.

*

Of course, it could be an elaborate trick. *Candid Camera* or so. After all, this was New York, second only to Los Angeles in making TV shows. It would be easy enough for a prepared production team to change the big clock in the lobby, maybe also somehow manipulate my cell phone. Emptying a restaurant full of extras would be just as easy.

Actually, I had been the victim of a Candid Camera setup in Sweden, when I was a high school kid. In downtown Stockholm, a boy no more than a couple of years younger than me was standing by an easel, making an oil painting of the Royal Palace. I was eager to have a look at it, since I was doing some painting myself.

His painting was almost finished. It was skilled, I found, but also rather boring. Too photographic for my taste, and too cowardly with the colors. It didn't occur to me for a second that this skill would be sensational.

Later, I saw on TV that it was a Candid Camera episode. A 'real' artist had made the painting beforehand. They edited me out of the show. I probably wasn't amazed enough.

What I experienced here at the Waldorf Astoria was much more amazing. Still, it could be a Candid Camera prank. That would explain a lot. Well, I got some Chateau Latour out of it. That was definitely real, my palate told me.

Since I didn't know anything for sure, yet, I decided just to go with it. But I would be more careful about what I said, from now on. I had no desire exposing myself intimately to millions of TV viewers. Perish the thought!

"We can't have that uncertainty," Cael objected and shook his head. "No more charade." Then he put his hand on my shoulder. "Think of a number, any number!"

I was about to laugh out loud. The typical party trick. But his demand still made me think of a number. It was kind of a reflex of the mind.

"Forty-seven," he said immediately.

It was correct. I had expected that he would instruct me to divide the number I thought of by two, add another number, and so on, before guessing it. That was usually how these tricks went. But he just got it at once. Not bad, I thought.

"Another one!"

As soon as I had decided on a new number, he said it aloud:

"Three. Again!"

I obliged, and again he answered at the very moment I had a number for him.

"Nineteen fifty-four. It's your birth year. Another!" This time, too, he said it as soon as I decided on it. "Pi. Let's not get into the numerals of it. Again!... A thousand-and-one. You were thinking of Arabian Nights. Wonderful stories. Again!... Eighty-three. Again!... Two-hundred eleven. Again!... Henry the Eighth. So, you're getting experimental. Again!..."

It was quick and he nailed it every time, although I wasn't completely faithful to the instruction he had given me.

"Okay," I said, interrupting this ping-pong. "You could have a Vegas show with that."

"I wanted you to understand that there is no point in holding back what you say, unless you can do that also with what you think."

"I doubt it. I have a hard enough time trying to think about nothing when I meditate," I said and offered him a smile. But I couldn't help thinking that this was all very much like some magic show, in Vegas or elsewhere.

He sighed, but smiled and lifted his hand from my shoulder.

"You're a tough one to convince, Stefan. Many others would panic into complete denial. Your vivid imagination is your protection. We'll see how far it takes you."

If it were not for his gentle smile, his words would seem like a threat.

Then he started walking towards the buffet, and I followed like a puppy. As we took our steps, I could see waiters leave the restaurant area. All the tables of the restaurant were still empty, so what else could they do? One by one, they disappeared from sight.

"We have no need for them," Cael said without turning to me.

The cooks at the buffet were still there, though. But the piano player got silent after finishing David Bowie's song. He stood up and walked away.

As I glanced at him leaving in the direction of the hotel foyer, it hit me that the reception was just as deserted as the restaurant. I saw no porter or receptionist, not a single hotel guest checking in or out. Except for me, Cael and the cooks at the buffet, the whole place was deserted.

We were surrounded by compact silence.

"Peaceful, isn't it?" Cael said, and there was that xylophone laugh of his again, playing a little jingle.

Somehow, it soothed me.

"How did you do that?" I had to ask.

Even a TV show would have great difficulty clearing the Waldorf Astoria lobby from people. Their hotel guests would hardly accept the inconvenience just to assist in some prank. Not with those prices.

"It's more like I undid," he replied. "We'll get to that. But first, let's have some more food. Aren't you still a little hungry?"

Strangely, I found that I was. It calmed me down some more. This couldn't be too crazy, since I still had an appetite.

*

Although I kept glancing now and then at the deserted surroundings, I managed to concentrate on the buffet. I thought of picking some more of the sliced ham, but then I found game on silver plates, both deer and moose. Rabbit, too. Had they been there before? I threw an eye at Cael. He just winked at me.

Our plates were rather full when we returned to our table. It had changed.

The table was slightly bigger than before, and the white cloth was fine linen with superb embroideries also in white. Our bottle remained, but the glasses had changed into even bigger and more elegant Bordeaux glasses. Our cutlery was shiny silver. Also, there was a chandelier with five lit candles to one side of the table, and a bouquet of orchids sticking up from a crystal vase on the other side. The chairs were new, as well. Their shapes were straighter, which I agreed with more, and their backrests stopped short of shoulder blade height. Also a plus for comfort.

Only when we were about to sit down, did I realize that the big black marble pillar adjacent to our table was gone. We had a free view of the whole restaurant and lobby area. It seemed we were right in the middle of it all.

Were it not for the Latour bottle, I would suspect we had walked up to another table of the Peacock Alley. Of course, moving a bottle of wine from one table to another would not be much of a feat, so it was certainly possible. But my sense of direction, such as it was, told me that we had returned to the same spot.

As we sat down, the light in the restaurant and the lobby dimmed. Only our table remained lit, but no more than so that the candle light had a chance of showing off.

Cael filled our glasses and raised his for a wordless toast. When they clung together, they gave a most clear sound, like church bells. Definitely crystal.

We drank. I took a couple of gulps. I needed it.

To my surprise, the taste of the wine was significantly more refined than I remembered from previous glasses of it. Sensationally so. My pallet marveled at it. The previous taste had been heavenly, but this was even more, if that is conceivable. Heaven right by God's feet.

I held the glass close to the white tablecloth and tilted it slightly. The wine's color had not changed, as far as I could tell. I checked the bottle. Cael observed me with what looked like a rascal smile.

It was still Chateau Latour, but the vintage was not 1998 anymore. It was legendary 2000, a sublime year for all Bordeaux reds. I looked up with widened eyes at Cael.

"Welcome to my world," he said calmly.

Destiny

I have always had a complicated relation to destiny – not really believing in it, but still having frequent impressions of perceiving traces of it. I have come to trust it without submitting to it. Although nothing can be said with certainty about the future, it is not impossible to predict, at least in glimpses.

How the past leads to a certain future is often visible, sort of like footsteps in the snow. You see where they came from and where they head. Although you see no starting point and no end, the direction is evident and you could simply follow them to get to wherever they lead. They will bring you there.

The future can at times be almost as evident as those footsteps in the snow. You know where you will end up if you follow that path. At other times it is much vaguer. Well, usually it is quite vague. Like those footsteps when the snow keeps falling.

But there are patterns to be detected. There always are. One thing leads to another, and so on. Life can seem chaotic at times and the future a mere toss of the dice. Still, when examined closely there is some kind of order and logic to it. We always see it in hindsight, which means we should be able to get some grasp of it already beforehand.

In a novel of mine – I forget which one – I described the patterns of destiny as the ticking of hidden relays, when they open or close. If you listen very attentively, you can hear that ticking. It is behind what we do, limiting our options, steering us along very discreetly.

They don't tick all the time. Usually, we just go ahead with our lives in a routine manner, forgetting one day when waking up to the next. Destiny is not involved, maybe even dormant. But when you hear that tick, you know a significant event is imminent.

That signal doesn't have to be anything very dramatic. I have found that it usually isn't. A sole letter in the mailbox. The phone ringing at a moment of unusual silence. A sudden rain making you take cover in a coffee shop you haven't visited before. Seemingly trivial things that still make you alert, without knowing why. That's the sound of the relays of destiny.

I don't have the impression that it is personal, although it certainly happens to you specifically when the relay ticks. You are sure to have a leading role in the event that follows. But all these relays are connected into one single machine, which is the world. The universe. Everything.

There is one symphony being played, involving all of us. And it has been playing since the dawn of time. Each life is a melody, which is part of that grand symphony. The music of the spheres, involving everything from microcosm to macrocosm.

Well, that's what it feels like. I must be kind of religious, after all.

*

Then again, maybe I am not. A lot of premonitions can be explained rationally. The past holds a lot of clues to the future. That is true on both a personal and a global level.

Some sciences excel at prediction. Others do not. Over all, most of them improve at it, as the years go by. Maybe we all do, regarding our own lives. We should, if we have learned anything along the way. So, maybe our sense of premonition is simply the conclusions we draw from our own growing experience.

No, there is more to it.

Of course we get better at predicting, when we learn more about ourselves and what surrounds us. But there is a limit to how far rational deduction can take us. It all depends on things along the way going as planned. No surprises.

Yet, if there is one thing we all quickly learn about life, it is that it's full of surprises. And they tend to come when and where we least expect them.

So, I believe in prediction, but I have limited trust in making plans. Most of them tend to fall apart because of what are called unforeseen circumstances. Can they be foreseen? It is my experience that they can, now and then. I've done it, repeatedly.

Since adolescence, I've experimented with occult and other methods of prediction. In the beginning I had my doubts, to say the least, but the results gradually convinced me to continue. My trust in them grew. I have used astrology with complete horoscope charts, not just the simplified Zodiac sign thing the newspapers settle for. Also Tarot divination cards, the *I Ching*, and briefly a little palmistry.

They all gave impressive results. So, what could I do but examine them further? Not that I ever got rid of gnawing doubts from the rational domain of my mind, but those doubts were losing evidence to support them.

Actually, I was more interested in the implications of prediction by such means at all being possible, than I was in what they could tell about my own future. I checked now and then, when I heard that ticking of the hidden relays, but I never had the patience to regularly predict my immediate future. I'm not even sure it would work to any significant degree.

Much like the relays of destiny, the methods of prediction deal with the big picture and the main events.

Still, the implications of it are indeed intriguing. It means that the future must in some way be fixed, as well as accessible. And this means that in a way, the future is already present in the now. Probably no less than the past is. What does that say about the universe?

With the Tarot cards, pure chance decides what cards will come up in a spread. It is the same with how the hexagrams are decided when the *I Ching* book is used. So, what this suggests is that there is no such thing as pure chance. Instead, it is a door to destiny.

If we can read what we call random occurrences correctly, they can be used to predict the future. Probably any random occurrences. They show how the world works when we don't interfere.

Astrology is a little different, since it is mainly based on the birth chart horoscope, which is the same for a person all through life. But it can be said that the positions of the planets at the moment of birth is a random setting. Then their ability to reveal something about a person's future is not because the planets are influencing it in some way, but just because they are completely unrelated to it. Haphazard.

We have it in our minds, too. We can create a state of mind with the ability to predict. That would be what is called premonition. It feels like something instinctual, apart from the rational way the conscious mind usually works when reaching for conclusions.

I don't know about others, but I have had such moments, ever since childhood. Well, they didn't make much sense to me until my late teens. Before that, I didn't have enough experience to understand how my premonitions might manifest themselves, what kinds of events they signaled in advance. Life was too much of a wondrous chaos before adolescence. Only then did I start to make plans for the future I had just dreamed about before that.

My guess is that we all experience premonitions, with differing frequencies. The question is how much we listen to them – and how much we can separate them from wishful thinking. It is hard for us to accept what we do not want or would not expect. Such glimpses of the future, we tend to ignore or outright deny.

The plans we make stand in the way of realizing them.

Many times I have been obnoxious towards destiny and the premonitions I got of the future. I saw where the footsteps in the snow were going, but I still decided to take another route.

I've found that you can do that, sometimes. It is possible to refuse destiny. I doubt that it is wise to do, but we can. Maybe we even need to, occasionally, just to keep at least a fraction of what is called the free will.

In my experience, it can't be done every time. Some things just happen as predicted, no matter how hard I try to resist. And it's not very clear why.

It's not necessarily the events that are the grandest, the seemingly most important ones. Actually, it's almost the other way around. Things that seem to be peripheral and insignificant prove to be impossible to avoid, whereas big life events are much more accessible to alterations.

I get the same impression from the ticks of the relays of destiny. They are discreet and often seemingly insignificant.

If there is some kind of grand plan of the universe and everything in it, that plan is executed through minute details and not by bombastic events. It is sort of a background thing, as if the major entity of the universe is in between all the stars and planets.

Of course, that is exactly what modern astronomy

claims. The greatest forces of the universe are dark matter and dark energy, invisible and impalpable, but absolutely instrumental.

Destiny works in the shadows of the alleys, not on the heavily trafficked main streets. That which forms the future is in the detail.

Big things come and go. They may be ever so spectacular, like fireworks, but their influence rarely lasts any longer than fireworks, in the overall perspective. They are just noise. Lao Tzu would agree.

*

Many of these little key events are truly unavoidable. They cannot be altered. Some of them, though, are not complete events, but opportunities. They appear with a tick of the relay, but if they are neglected they go away. And that's it.

I have had such experiences. Those are the moments of my life I regret the most. By insensitivity or ignorance, I let wonderful opportunities slip away. It was almost always because I had made other plans and imagined that it was important to stick to them. Plans really are foolish.

Mostly, these instances have involved other people. Strangers I met by chance, as we like to call it. People are major instruments of destiny, at least to other people. At least. There may be much more to us than that.

Usually, I take delight in meeting and getting to know other people. I can become like a leech, sticking to them and sucking the essence out of them – who they are, what they think and dream. Well, what makes them tick. I want to scrutinize them to the core.

Frankly, people are sort of lab rats to me. I dissect them in my continuous effort to understand mankind and thereby myself. It's a quest of mine. Maybe it's all about me.

Still, it has happened sometimes that I neglected the opportunity to get to know someone who appeared before me, with that discreet signal of carrying a valuable clue to what we are all about. There have been times when I just moved on, leaving that person behind and ignoring what I might have discovered, because I was busy with something else.

I still remember those encounters, and I still regret them.

The first time it happened, I was in my late teens. I had reached the age when I started to be aware of the patterns of destiny, the discreet ticking of its relays. In spite of that, I missed the chance and I regret it ever since.

It was late one rather cold autumn evening, when I got to a bus stop after an aikido class. Another boy was standing there waiting for the bus, which was soon to arrive. We greeted each other with casual nods, but there was something in his eyes as he not only watched me, but gazed at me. It was as if he expected something from me, although we were strangers.

It bothered me, but I shook it off. I said something cheerful and utterly meaningless, whatever it was. He still waited.

The bus came and I stepped aboard, thinking that the other boy would surely do the same. In the suburb where I lived, buses were scarce, especially at night, so he must have waited for the same one.

But when the door closed and the bus started moving, he was still standing by the bus stop, gazing at me as I sat down. The warmth and light in the bus was a stark contrast to the darkness and cold where he stood.

Our eyes were connected until he disappeared out of view.

I had no idea of what I had missed, but I knew it was

an opportunity. Something intriguing, something significant. As my frustration grew, I promised myself never to be that negligent again. Mostly, I have kept that promise. Mostly.

So, of course I had perceived the ticking of destiny's relays when Cael appeared before me at the Waldorf Astoria Sunday brunch. His striking looks alone made my alarm go off. He sure didn't disappoint me.

As he sat there on the other side of the table, the flickering candle light playing with the features of his face, I had to smile at my fortune. This meeting – destined, since it happened by chance – was so much more rewarding than anything the brunch buffet had to offer.

It even surpassed the superb bouquet of the Chateau Latour in my glass, of which I had another delightful sip.

"It is mutual," Cael said, returning my smile, "or it would not have happened."

Revelation

I had eaten most of the meat on my plate. So had Cael. Lifting my glass, I leaned back in my chair and took a sip of the tremendous wine. I kept the glass close to my lips. I felt quite comfortable, in spite of the many strange things that had just happened.

"So, Cael, what's all this about?"

"That's the right question," he replied as a grin spread over his face. "It's about you, of course."

"Well, it certainly has been, so far," I said, shrugging my shoulders. "I thought it was your turn, now."

"I," he started, pointing himself in the chest, and then turning his finger to aim at me, "will tell you all."

He followed it up immediately with his xylophone laughter. This was beginning to feel like a game kids play. Hide and seek of sorts. Was Cael just doing everything he could to avoid being the subject of our conversation?

That was what he had done so far, quite successfully. His repeated assurances of telling me all about him might have been no more than tricks to keep me talking about myself.

On the other hand, I could not claim to have been displeased with the conversation up to this point. But it was time Cael lived up to his promise. I had become unbearably curious about him. His magic show the last few minutes – however he had done it – set fire to the enigma. I needed to get some answers.

"I am the one who made all this," he said and made a sweeping gesture at our surroundings.

"All the tricks? Well, duh. Who else? The question is how you did it."

"Not just that. All."

"The Waldorf Astoria? It was built in the nineteen-thirties. Even if you refer to the renovation in the eighties, you're far from old enough."

"There you go with time, again. It has no meaning." He shook his head. "I mean all. Not just this place, nor this city or continent. Not only this particular planet, this solar system and galaxy. All."

There was a moment of silence. I stared at him.

"Did you just say that you created the universe? You have to do more than a few magic tricks to convince me of that."

To my surprise, I realized when saying it that I hoped he would. I shook my head at my own folly.

"You're a hard man to convince," Cael said, with the corners of his mouth curving upwards. "Your own imagination is lively enough to find explanations for just about everything."

"If you made everything, you must have some really spectacular trick up your sleeve."

"I'm not so fond of disrupting my own world order. You with your knowledge of Taoism must understand that."

"Didn't you just stop time?" I checked the big clock. It was still a quarter to twelve.

"I've already told you..." Cael started.

"Time has no meaning. Yes, you've made that clear."

"But you think it's some trick that anyone can make with a little preparation."

I nodded.

"You can see my problem. I stopped time for you, and still you're not convinced. So, what do I have to do?"

"Something that can't be done by human beings."

"Can you stop time?"

"No, but I can stop clocks."

Cael laughed again. Although he complained about my lack of faith, he seemed to enjoy it quite a lot.

"How about this, then?"

*

He had not moved at all. He just sat there, waiting for my reaction. I looked around but could not see that anything at all had changed. When my eyes returned to Cael, he was grinning from ear to ear.

"You'll enjoy this one," he said and took a sip from his wine glass.

"Enjoy what? I don't see anything."

Cael put the glass back on the table, rather slowly, before replying.

"Where haven't you looked yet?"

Again I let my eyes search around the Peacock Alley and the hotel lobby. I even looked up at the ceiling. Nothing.

"Stefan, you disappoint me. It's not much of a riddle."

My mind struggled for another few seconds before it hit me.

"You've changed me!"

I looked down on my body and my hands in front of me. My clothes were the same, but my hands seemed more slim than usual and the skin on them smoother. Also, my belly did not bulge at all, as if I had suddenly lost a lot of weight.

I put on my glasses and picked up my cell phone to turn on its camera.

To my surprise, my vision was blurry. I blinked a few times, but it did not change. I couldn't see the display of the phone sharply, whether I moved it closer to my eyes or extended my arm to increase the distance.

I took the glasses off again to check if the lenses were smudged. As I did so, I could suddenly see everything clearly. The cell phone display, Cael on the other side of the table, everything around me. It was all sharper than ever before.

It dawned on me just how Cael had changed me. I turned on the cell phone camera, switched to the lens on the display side, and held it up in front of me, as if taking a selfie. I could see my face clearly. It had certainly changed. I stared into the face of a young man, about the same age as Cael.

It didn't take me more than a couple of seconds to recognize the face. It was mine, but as it had been when I was that age. My hair was brown instead of gray. My eyes were so dark brown the irises were hardly distinguishable from the pupils. My ears and nose were visibly smaller, my skin was smooth and the bags under my eyes were gone. I tried a smile. It was awkward, but my teeth were snow white.

I had become me when I was about twenty. Long time no see...

"Oh Cael," I said with a sigh. "You're playing with my heart."

*

Aging is no picnic. All the way until I got to be fifty, I had the confidence of an immortal. Then it dawned on me that there was a downward slope ahead, with an unavoidable ending. What happened to everyone else would happen to me, too. Of course, I had always known it, so to say intellectually. But that is far from the same as accepting it and feeling it. At fifty I did.

Life is a cruel joke. Once you get used to it and really start forming it to your own liking, it prepares for its departure. Like a poker player at an all-in, raking in the pot and sneaking away, just as you are about to show your winning hand. You can't win.

I can understand the desperate need for a belief in the afterlife. How else to have a sense of meaning with life? If it ends when you have finally learned how to deal with it – what's the point? Wisdom wasted, experience discarded.

Whatever we try to tell ourselves, it is simply so that if life has an end date, then so has the meaning of it.

My favorite solace is the idea that what one individual might sow, the following generations might reap. Each man perishes, but mankind moves on.

It is a nice principle, I think. We are all in it for everybody else. A natural law of altruism. And it might be true.

Or not.

In any case, it is no perfect cure for the despair we all feel deep at heart, before the death we face. It is the wormwood tainting our days from birth and on. The shadow that no light can erase, not even momentarily.

When I was still young, maybe at the age to which Cael had now made my body return, it hit me that just about every human folly comes from the fact that we will die and we know it. It makes us desperate and pushes us to actions and behaviors that sanity would not allow.

That's why people disgrace themselves and sometimes even strike at others to get ahead. It's why some chase power or money and then use it to glorify themselves at the huge cost of others. It tricks us to suffer all kinds of ordeals in the hope of a reward, even if it doesn't come until mere minutes before our last breath.

And it's what makes parents force their children to take other paths in life than their own curiosities would pick. As if their lives would rewrite those of their parents.

The maddest things we do stem from our longing to live forever, in one way or other.

That also goes for the sweet idea of doing good for mankind. It's just another way of striving for immortality. Still a good idea, I'd say. But let's not kid ourselves. We struggle for significance that defeats time.

Aren't we all clowns?

*

But Cael's turning me into the youth of my distant past also tore at my heart for more personal reasons, which hurt even more. The decay I had gone through since that time, what had I done with my life to make it worthwhile?

The graying hair. The increased weight gathering where it was the least flattering to my body. The sense of fatigue gradually but surely gnawing on my active hours. The prolonged distances between moments of enthusiasm and delight. For short: the years. How had I used them?

Sure, I had written a number of books, some of which I was quite proud, none of them I regretted. I had gotten skilled at aikido, even in the sort of magic that attracted me to it. I had experienced things, met loads of people, and learned tons of things that probably made me wiser.

I had even loved, occasionally.

Although I had accomplished things that I was proud of, each passing year reminded me of the many days, weeks and maybe even months or years, which I had wasted on meaningless things, in the foolish belief of having – as Cael had put it – all the time. Would the young me be pleased?

I doubted it. Actually, I was quite sure that if I had continued to listen to him, there would have been more of an urge to my life. A healthy impatience, a creative persistence. As it was, the young me would have found reason to accuse me of being lazy. He would not be wrong.

He might have been unrealistic. But not wrong. I could have done more.

Honestly, I missed him. Suddenly again carrying his light body and looking at his untarnished face through the display of my cell phone, I was overcome by a sadness like that of a lost love. I had not always been proud of him, even back then, but I did love him.

Even in regard to myself, I was right about love not lasting. Well, I still loved him, the Stefan of my youth. I had a harder time loving the aging version. In ways I did not care to recollect, he had disappointed me along the ride that is a lifetime unfolding.

I had to sigh, although Cael was bound to hear it.

It took me a while to tear my eyes from the face in the display. But before I did, I took a picture. Then I made sure that it was indeed in the cell phone album. Again I had trouble looking away. I blinked hard as I put the phone back in my pocket. My eyes were moistening.

Time, which Cael claimed has no meaning – it sure passes quickly. Not the minutes or the hours. They can linger. But the years. Where did they go?

"Do you want to remain like that?" Cael asked. His voice was very gentle.

"I want to, I must confess. But it's a bad idea. Alas! Please don't ask me to elaborate."

"I won't."

I could feel my weight return to normal, pressing heavily on the chair, and I saw my hands resume their present age. I had no urge to pick up the cell phone again to check my face.

"Sorry to upset you, Stefan."

"I asked for it."

"You did. So, are you convinced?"

"I'm convinced that you can do what no human being can."

He played his xylophone.

"So far so good," he said. "That will do for now."

Dreaming

We were simply looking at each other for a while. None was eating anymore, although we both had something left on our plates. The wine, though, we kept on enjoying. In my case, almost ecstatically.

"We've established you're not human," I said, adding a quick smile as sort of a shield against the absurdity. "So, what are you? A space alien?"

"If that's your first guess, you're not as religious as you might think."

"Some kind of god, then?"

"I don't even know what that means."

"Nor do I, really. What then?"

"To quote a text you're familiar with, 'I am who I am.'"

"Ah, what God said to Moses when asked about his name. A name worth contemplating. Anyone uttering it makes himself like God. So it became blasphemy. That's how the rabbis got to Jesus. He said it and they demanded that he be executed for blasphemy."

"That's just it."

"You're Jesus?"

He shook his head. I was not surprised. I merely asked the question to make him clarify.

"That name of God can be rightly used by anyone. I am who I am. Who is not?"

"Then the question is: who is that? We don't really know who we are, fundamentally. That's no clearer to us than who God might be."

"What does that tell you?"

"We're all the same?"

"Can you change yourself the way I just did?"

"Well, there's plastic surgery..."

He rewarded me with his xylophone, but just a few notes of it. I had to give the question some serious thought. Cael refilled our glasses and waited patiently.

"Well," I started hesitantly, "I guess we enter Descartes' territory. We think, therefore we are. That's about all we know for certain, each one of us on our own. Someone thinks, someone wonders what is. That thought, then, is proven to exist. Because I think it, I know I exist, whatever it is I am. Everything else is uncertain. So, I guess the proper name for us all would be I am whoever I am."

"Which says a lot."

"Indeed. All we know about the world is what our thoughts suggest to us. It might as well be a dream."

Cael nodded, but then just waited for me to continue. We were still doing the monologue thing, in spite of his promises. But my mind was happily spinning on these existential questions, so I didn't care – for now.

"Chuang Tzu, the other great Taoist, played with the idea in the famous butterfly story. He dreamed about being a butterfly. When he woke up to be himself again, he was not sure if it was instead the butterfly dreaming of being him. Either the butterfly was a figment of his imagination, or he was imagined by the butterfly. There was no way of knowing."

"Or both."

Again I had to pause momentarily, staring at Cael, before answering.

"I guess that would be possible, too," I said without feeling the least bit sure. "We could both exist, dreaming about being the other. But one thing is sure: At least one of us has to exist, or we are back to that impossible nothing and denying Descartes' claim."

"That would get us nowhere," Cael replied with a swift smile.

I chuckled.

"Nothing gets us nowhere," I added. "How about you, Cael? Are you Chuang Tzu or the butterfly?"

"I dream both."

"So do I. We all dream each other. Once I become aware of someone, that person is in my memory, accessible to my dreams and thoughts. Whether that's where the person was born to begin with is something very difficult to disprove completely. Maybe everyone else only exists in my imagination. Maybe this is all just a dream of mine. If I pinch myself I wake up and find I'm all alone in the void."

"Try it."

"Oh, life deals us far worse blows than mere pinches. I would surely have woken up by now, if that were the case. No, this is real."

I knocked on the table, just to illustrate in some way what I said. The tablecloth muffled the sound.

"I don't doubt it for a moment. The world outside me is there, and not just in my head. But that doesn't mean I know its true nature. That remains a mystery. Feel free to fill in the blanks."

I met his eyes, but before he had the time to give any reply, I continued with a question.

"Are you the one dreaming all of this?"

"It's all real," Cael stated quite firmly. "I made it so."

"That makes sense. If I were but a figure in your dream, how could I be thinking? How could I wonder in my mind who you are? And I do, more and more."

He was amused, but not showing any need to talk. He probably knew I had more objections. So I continued.

"But Cael, how can you be present in your own creation? You can't be both the creator and part of that creation."

His eyebrows jumped up, as if by surprise.

"Oh, this is not me," he said, pointing at his chest and shaking his head. "This is just an appearance I use to communicate comfortably with you. Comfortably for both of us."

To my surprise, I felt disappointment. It would mean that this young man in front of me was nothing more than a phantasm, a dummy of sorts. What a pity.

"Don't get me wrong. Like everything I make, it is still real. It's not me, but it is flesh and blood. You can feel it."

He reached over and grabbed my free hand, resting on the table. I remembered the sensation from our initial handshake. His skin was warm and so dry, it gave a tickling sensation. It was very pleasant. My disappointment was gone. I hoped that he would never let go.

"Is it possible to see what you really look like?" I wondered, quickly adding, "Probably not, if we are from different worlds."

"You're right. That's not how it works. I don't look like something at all. Eyes can't see me, ears can't hear me. That's why I use this body. I can give it any shape. Do you want me to change it?"

I had to smile.

"You look fine the way you are. And I've gotten used to it."

He let go of my hand. I held back a sigh. Then I looked at my hand, as if expecting it to have turned into gold or something. It had not.

"You still doubt me, don't you?" He didn't seem offended or bothered at all. He said it neutrally, merely stating a fact. The question was rhetorical.

"I've seen what you can do. No doubt about that. And surely you can do other things that would amaze me even more. But did you make the whole world? That, I will continue to doubt until it's not possible anymore. Of course."

"Of course," he repeated. Now it was his time to smile.

"Until then I am fine with regarding this conversation as hypothetical. It doesn't make it any less interesting to me, I assure you. So let's go on, if you don't mind."

"I don't mind."

*

"I'd like to hear you explain how you went about making this world. But before that – where are you, if not here, and did someone or something make you?"

Cael leaned back in his chair, took a sip from his wine glass and kept holding it up in front of him, staring sort of dreamy into its red content.

"The first question is easy. I am everywhere. Here and elsewhere. There is nowhere I am not."

"As if the whole world is your body?"

"Part of my body. Or, to be more precise, my mind."

"The universe exists only in your imagination?"

He sort of giggled, but made no sound.

"There is no only about it. And I've already told you it's all real. Just like my money. Your understanding of imagination is flawed, but we will get to that."

He paused shortly.

"Your second question is not that easy to answer."

"So I figured," I butted in teasingly.

"When I said I am everywhere, it also means at every time. Time is not a stopwatch that was started at some point and is stopped at another. It is one of the conditions of existence, which has to have a when as well as a where. The where is everywhere and the when is everywhen, if that's a word. Otherwise it could not exist at all."

"I think a bunch of the old Greek philosophers would agree with you there," I said. "I guess it's all about how the universe is to be defined. Is it the expanding space we can observe, presumably born in a Big Bang, or is it that in which it was able to appear?"

He flashed me a quick smile, peeking at me from behind the glass he was still holding up.

"Something like that. I am everywhere and everywhen. So, I am inseparable from whatever you can see – and a lot that you can't. In that sense, I was not made. There is no where and when out of which I could have emerged."

"In that sense? So, in some other sense you were made by someone or something?"

"That's the difficult part."

"You don't say?"

I allowed myself a short laugh, wishing it had the same melodic quality as Cael's. He was kind enough not to make that obvious by letting his laugh out.

"I was made by the world I made."

He paused momentarily to give me a chance to comment, but I was satisfied with waiting for him to continue. I wouldn't know what to say, anyway.

"The world could not be without a maker, and a maker could not be without a world made."

"Ah, I think again some Greek philosophers would agree with you. Was it Plato who claimed that the world must have a maker, or it would be imperfect – at least incomplete?"

Cael shrugged his shoulders. He was not inclined to discuss the Greek philosophers. Well, he did have his own idea about it.

"That's the misconception of time, again," he said. "I

am the world maker, but it is not something of the past. There was no moment when I made the world, and that was it. I make it always and everywhere. No beginning, no end. It is all now. Here and now."

"Wait a minute," I interjected. "You've used the past tense about it, earlier in our conversation. As late as just a minute ago."

"Language has its limits. I've tried not to be cryptic."

"Nice try," I said with a chuckle. "So, it's like the Japanese expression 'nakaima,' then. Right in the middle of just now. Here and now. I remember my Japanese aikido teacher back in the day explaining it as a term suggesting Paradise, heavenly bliss. Where we all should try to be."

"We all are."

"In Paradise? That can be discussed."

"Here and now. Not even in your dreams are you able to be anywhere else."

After thinking about it for just a few seconds I had to agree with him on that. In no dream of mine I could remember had I been in the past or the future. Dreams are always in the present, whatever the setting and whatever happens.

"But my memories can take me back," I objected. "And I can at least plan for the future, even imagine it."

"You don't believe in planning for the future."

I was going to ask him how he knew that, but skipped it. Another trick up his sleeve. Or had I mentioned it?

"I am sure I can, although I don't expect it to come true."

"So, it's not the future. Just the illusion of it."

"But when I remember the past, sometimes as vividly as if actually revisiting it, I relate to something real, something that really happened."

Cael returned his glass to the table and leaned forward.

"As a writer and journalist, you know to question your sources, don't you?"

I only had time to nod, before he continued.

"Then surely you have done the same with your memories, occasionally. Have you found them accurate?"

"Some of them."

"Perhaps not the ones you checked properly?"

"Perhaps," I reluctantly admitted. "My memory mixes up details and gets things wrong. But it catches sort of the overall picture. Well, I have to say that sometimes I get it completely wrong. We're not computers. We forget."

"It's not that you forget. It's that memories have no meaning on their own. They relate to the present, which interprets them according to the situation. They are fabrications. The past cannot be relived. Otherwise it would not be the past."

"But you can't deny I have a past. All of us do. Even you, surely. I've been a child, I grew up, I've gone through things during the years I have lived."

"No, you haven't."

I sighed audibly, not to say demonstratively.

"Yes I have. I didn't appear out of nowhere, just for this Sunday brunch."

"That child wasn't you. You're different. Your connection to that child is lost. You are no closer to him than you are to other people around you. Even less so. It's even true about the Stefan who boarded the airplane in Copenhagen just the other day to fly here. None of them is you."

"Sure, that's one way of looking at it. The river in Herman Hesse's book about Siddharta. The river remains but is never the same, since water streams through it constantly. But the riverbed keeps its shape. And I go through life in this body of mine. Experiences change my mind, but my mind keeps on being contained in this body."

I even clapped my chest a couple of times to illustrate my words. It almost made me cough.

"Come now, Stefan. You know enough biology to realize that's not true. Your body changes as much as Siddharta's river does. Compare to you as a child. The size alone is vastly different. And inside your body there is constant change in a multitude of ways. Your body doesn't stay the same even from one minute to the next."

"But it's my body. It doesn't change into someone else's."

I had raised my voice. I was getting irritated by what seemed more and more like a play on words. We were talking past each other. I hate when that happens. It is pointless and leads nowhere.

"It is far from pointless," Cael protested, while still keeping his voice as low as before.

That mind reading of his! I might have let out a grunt.

"I want you to consider what it suggests about who you are," he continued. "Instead of seeing yourself as a vessel going from the place of your birth to your final destination, slowly deteriorating on the way, look at it from here and now. Everything is changing around you. What you call your past is changing, as is what you call your future. Your body, too. In the middle of all that, the very middle – that's where you are. Nowhere else."

"Sure," I said. "That's one way of putting it."

"That's how it is. When I changed your body to that of the adolescent Stefan, you didn't see it at first. And when you did discover it, you were also aware of yourself remaining the same inside that alternate body. You knew that you and that body were not the same. There you are, in the middle of all that change. In the eye of the hurricane."

"But my mind has changed, too, over the years. The way I see myself."

"Has it really?"

"Yes!" I insisted. "I think differently now, also about myself. It's still me, of course, but I have matured or whatever." I knew at the moment I said it that I was not so sure. I corrected myself, "At least I have acquired some skills along the way."

He showed me his shiny white teeth in a smile. It was contagious.

"You know what I mean," I said with a little sigh.

"I also know that you don't mean it."

"What a surprise," I muttered. But I could not confidently deny it.

"You are familiar with that absolute core within yourself, which is the same through all the changes. You know that you are who you are. You can adapt to circumstances. You can pretend, too. But all through, you are who you are. That doesn't change. It can't. Because it's here and now, and that's all there is."

*

It bothered me, but I had to confess to myself that he was right. I have always had a sense of an unchanging me in the midst of it all, as if never moving an inch or aging a single minute. A clear and undeniable feeling of who I am, whom I address when I think about me.

It is the same one it was as far back as I can remember. As if my life had been nothing but a movie I was watching.

When I was a kid of ten or so, I had a peculiar recurring dream. It happened now and then, usually with several months in between, maybe more. This went on for a few years, I guess. It was not exactly a nightmare, but there was something ghastly about it, waking me up every time I had it.

Not much of a dream, since it was not a chain of events, adventures and such. It was more like a feeling, but with the very physical sensation by which dreams express themselves.

This was it, as far as my memory recalls:

I was in the very middle of my head, my skull, which was completely empty except for me in the middle of it. And the skull grew, or I shrunk – or both. Hard to tell. I remained in the middle of my skull, but the empty space around me got bigger and bigger. The sensation was painful, as if an increasing vacuum pulled at me.

I didn't explode or anything. I just remained there in the middle, somehow suffering from the expansion of the space around me, as my skull got bigger. An ache of sorts. The pain of a void. I don't know.

It was a mystery to me back then, and it still is. Neither the nature nor the shape of me in the middle of that space was detectable, sort of the same way you can't see yourself without a mirror. And I was unable to figure out how I could be in the middle of my own skull, as if we were two though yet just one.

When I was having that dream, I knew it said something fundamental about me, about who I am. But when I woke up I couldn't figure it out.

I was sure the truth was in the feeling, not the imagery. That expansion inside of me and around me at the same time. The suction of it, the vertigo of the paradox. It was who or what I really was. That I knew, somehow, when waking up.

But no matter how I tried, I couldn't catch its essence, the explanation hiding in the experience, although I was sure it would be evident once I got hold of it. If I could get the same feeling of that expansion in my head when awake, then I would know. I would know. But alas, it always escaped me just barely, teasingly, when I tried to grasp and sense it the minutes after it woke me up.

It was not only the mental difference between dreaming and being awake playing this trick on me. I was sure of that already at ten, when I started getting those dreams.

Well, maybe I had them long before that. I'm not sure. I had some weird dreams as far back as I can remember. And were they ever vivid – also when waking up from them!

Anyway, the nature of this dream, this feeling, was not so elusive only because it was a dream. It was mainly because of what it said about my existence, the essence of my being. I couldn't put it into words as a child, but I knew it.

If I could recapture that sensation when awake, I would understand exactly who I was, what it was to exist, to be. But I couldn't.

The dream has haunted me since. Not by returning. I haven't had it even once since those years long ago. But it happens now and then that I am reminded of it, and try again to grasp that sensation. I fail with an almost as small margin as back then. It is right outside my reach.

What remains is the very strong conviction that if I solve this riddle, reveal this enigma, I will know everything that really matters. The core, the all.

Strangely – and I don't know if it is significant – I seem to remember this:

In my dream, when I experienced that expanding skull of mine around me, I was sitting on a chair. But I'm not sure of the memory, and I have no clue at all as to what it would signify.

Was the chair what made me immovable in that middle? I did feel stuck in it, for sure. But again, I'm not sure about the chair.

"Was it comfortable?"

I snapped out of my thoughts and looked up at Cael, who was leaning very close to me, looking right into my eyes.

"The chair," he clarified. "Was it comfortable to sit on?"

It took me a little while to realize just how deep his mind reading was this time. The memories had made me doze off. My thoughts had been very far from that sort of superficial monologue one has in one's rational mind, with coherent words and sharp images. This had been a plunge deep into memories of my past.

"There is no past, remember?" Cael said mockingly. "So, was it?"

"Comfortable? Not at all, if I'm to trust my memory. It was awkward to sit on. I felt stuck on it."

Cael leaned even closer, keeping his eyes fixed on mine.

"Get up from that chair!" he whispered, but with an emphasis that made it sound like the hissing of a serpent.

Involuntarily, I recoiled. My legs tensed in an impulse to stand up, which I just barely managed to halt. Looking at him from the added distance, I expected him to show his teeth and play that xylophone again.

He didn't.

The How

I knew I would have to ponder that for quite some time. Maybe years. Yet, from the moment Cael uttered his surprisingly sharp command, I was convinced that I would do it.

I would get out of that chair. I would grasp the meaning of the childhood dream that kept on haunting me. It could take years or it could happen during our conversation at the Waldorf Astoria, where time had ceased to move.

Whenever, wherever – it would happen. I had no doubt of it. And this conviction made me relieved. Finally, the solution to that old enigma was within my reach.

But I had the perfect excuse to postpone it for now.

"Again, we're back at me," I complained. "You promised it was your turn now, Cael. So, please explain to me: You said that you make the world continuously, without a starting point. Always. That's the when. But what about the how? How do you go about making the world?"

He leaned back to a straight posture on his chair, but his eyes were still fixed on mine.

"I take it you're not going to stand up just yet," he teased me. "But we both know you will. Soon."

I nodded. The gravity of what that would mean weighed heavily on my shoulders. I felt some trepidation as well, since I sensed that Cael was not going to let me postpone it beyond our brunch. On the other hand, with time at a standstill, who knew how long this brunch would last?

I found that absurdity funny, which brought the inkling of a smile back to my face.

"I will try to answer," Cael continued. "But there is very little difference between the when and the how. If you understand one, you know the other."

"So, try me."

He let out a long 'hmm' while his eyes scrutinized my whole face, as if searching it for a clue to something. As if the answer to my question would be written on it and he wondered how to get me to realize that.

"Well," he started in a drawling manner and paused shortly before continuing. "The time is now and the place is here. We've been through that, right?"

I nodded, getting a little impatient.

"The how is similar. Since there is no past and no future, just the now, the how can't be a process over time. No chain of events, no elaborate construction from the ground up or from the core to the shell. Everything is just there." He chuckled very shortly and corrected himself. "I mean here."

"It's instant, that's what you say? Like a photo, painting the whole picture in one click."

"There isn't really any click."

"Of course. That would suggest a starting point. Your picture, on the other hand, is eternal." As he opened his mouth to respond, I hurried to add: "In the now."

He smiled.

"You're starting to get it."

"Not really," I replied, shaking my head slightly.

*

"Let's try it this way," Cael said, holding up his index finger. "There is nothing and there is something, completely separate from one another. Nothing is just nothing, absolutely nothing. But something is really everything. It can't be any less."

"Not if it's seen as the opposite of nothing, it can't."

"And it has to be. Everything that isn't nothing is something. Either there is the one or the other. It can't be a mix of them. So, nothing or everything."

"That's one way of looking at it," I commented with a smile meant to be teasing.

"So, humor me," Cael responded cheerfully.

I had another sip of the wine. It still had the ability to distract me with its overwhelming refinement. For a moment I forgot our strange conversation, the deserted restaurant and hotel lobby, even all the unbelievable things that had happened up to this point. I was sailing away on the Latour ocean. Only when Cael spoke again did I snap out of it.

"The how is the constant movement of everything. I make the world by stirring this constant flow into swirls. I make it dance."

He held up his hands and started moving them about in graceful sweeps, like flags fluttering in the wind or the elongated fins of veiltail goldfish as they swim in the aquarium.

It soon struck me that his hand movements were similar to mine, when I had tried to illustrate the nature of aikido.

He kept his hands going, and I started to be aware of the air between them. It was like I was able to see how it was affected by his sweeping hands. It gradually became clearer, as if the air was slowly turning into water. Cael created swirls in the air, which grew until they surrounded the hands, then the space between us, then beyond.

Soon, I saw it almost as clearly as waves on the surface of a sea. My chest was hesitant to inhale. I had to use a conscious effort to keep breathing. Probably, my instinct feared I had plunged into water.

Oddly, though, when I exhaled it had no effect on the swirls emanating from Cael's hand movements. I could see the air as I sucked it in, but not when I was breathing out. I wondered what it was doing inside of me, that swirling.

My eyes returned to Cael's hands, whereas he was looking directly at me. Now, the hands moved in a more complex pattern, which seemed to defy the agility of their joints. It was like they had melted into a liquid, but still kept their shape. The fingers moved completely independently of one another, the hands were no longer bound by the limitations of the wrists. They swirled much like the air around them, until it was no longer possible to see if they created the swirls or were moved by them.

The patterns got more and more detailed. Swirls within swirls within swirls. My eyes were drawn to the space between his hands, where the intricate movement of the air got increasingly precise as it seemed to slow down.

It looked like the air tightened into a fixed figure of those swirls within swirls. It didn't stop completely, maybe it did not even slow down. But the details of its slowly changing pattern became visible.

Soon, I thought I saw contours emerging in the dance of the air between Cael's hands. The contours were not fixed, but the continuous movement seemed to suggest and repeat them.

"This is the fabric of reality," Cael explained, continuing to move his hands in that strangely floating way.

I didn't even glance at his face when he spoke. My eyes were fixed on that visible air between his hands, where something was about to take shape, still just hinted by the patterns of all those swirls.

Something was forming out of the air. It was kind of spherical, filling out the space between Cael's hands. He increased the distance until the hands were almost three feet apart. The sphere swelled to fill that gap. The number of swirls increased and slowed down.

I wasn't sure about it, but that was the impression I got. The surface of the sphere got more visible and its shape changed, extending here, contracting there, like clay being formed into a figure.

The more I noticed this, the quicker the transformation happened. The something that was formed got a definite shape and its surface thickened until its interior was invisible. Then color, then sharpness and details all over.

I found myself looking at a big bird floating in the space between Cael's hands. I recognized it from old drawings in history books. It was a dodo, the bird that got extinct in the 17th century. There it was, floating in the air, its round body, stubby wings, oddly shaped beak and all.

Cael gently separated his hands even more and let them land on the table. So did the dodo bird, slowly. When its feet weighed solidly on the white tablecloth, the bird looked at me, turned its head to the side, opened its beak and quacked like a duck.

"You're a funny guy, Cael," I mumbled.

He responded with his xylophone laughter. It made the dodo turn to him and let out another quack.

"You created it out of thin air."

Cael shook his head.

"I made it with the swirls. Air was not needed. It just tagged along, you can say." He was soon to add, "I didn't really make it. It was there in the swirls all along. Everything is. I just brought it forward."

I stared at the odd creature. It looked back at me with its round eyes, tilting its head left and right but keeping its eyes on me.

"Touch it!" Cael urged me.

"Won't it bite me if I do?" I asked, looking with respect at the big beak with its curved pointed tip. It was like a hook.

"No, it won't."

I thought the one who made the bird would know, but still I felt some anxiety when I extended my index finger to touch the dodo ever so lightly on the side. The bird didn't react at all. It didn't even bother to look at my finger.

"Come on," Cael said. "Put your whole hand on it."

I did. I laid my hand gently on the dodo's back. I could feel the warmth of its body. Still, it didn't seem to mind at all.

"Relax. Let your hand rest there."

I obeyed. It took me a little while to relax, but when I did I could feel movement inside the bird's body. Was that its pulse?

Cael shook his head. It must have been in response to my thought.

Gradually, I could relax my hand even more. Then the feeling got more distinct. Although the body of the dodo was definitely solid, I could feel movement, as if it was a liquid contained inside a thin cover. It yielded to my touch, and that movement increased. It was swirling, just like the air had been when slowly forming into the dodo.

Under my hand's touch, the swirling increased and then I saw the whole dodo begin to lose its fixed shape, as if melting. Gravity was discretely pulling my hand downwards, and the body of the bird gave in. My hand was slowly sinking through the dodo, which dissolved in the process.

Soon, my hand was on the table and the dodo was gone. I saw nothing more than the swirling air where the bird had been. After a little while, that had also faded away, and I was looking right into Cael's face on the other side of the table.

"That is how," he said. Then he smiled.

I could not. I had to lift my hand and look at it, as if traces of what had happened would remain there. A feather or so. But nothing.

*

After a couple of gulps of the wine, I decided to voice some objections about Cael's explanation. I had a feeling it was a bad idea, but I couldn't resist.

"If that's how you created the world, it must have taken forever. Only that dodo took a couple of minutes to appear."

"I told you time is not an issue," Cael replied immediately. Maybe his voice revealed some impatience with me.

It got darker around us and I became aware of a big shadow above our heads. I turned my head up and gasped.

A giant hairy mammoth was hovering above us. It was upside down, but it didn't seem to mind. Its curved tusks were long enough to give any elephant nightmares. Me too, of course.

"You won't let it down, will you?" I asked, more concerned than I wanted him to notice.

Next instant, the mammoth was gone. A sigh of relief escaped me. At the same time I noticed swirls in the air where the big animal had been. Then they disappeared, too.

"Cael, you have a strange sense of humor," I mumbled. "This is getting absurd."

Cael grinned at me. He seemed to be in a good mood again, fortunately. I decided to be more careful with my objections. He laughed.

"That fabric of reality I showed you is everywhere and contains everything. I didn't create the dodo and the mammoth. I just showed them. They were already there.

They still are, like everything else."

"Am I made up of the same stuff?" I asked, and then hurried to add, "Please don't show me! Just tell me."

"Yes," he said plainly, but with great amusement. "You are within it."

"Are you?"

"This is," he replied, pointing towards his chest. "But I am elsewhere." He paused and took a look at me before he continued. "Actually, and you're probably not going to like this – I am nowhere."

I frowned.

"You know what I think about that."

"I know, Stefan. But you asked. And mind you, I said nowhere. Not nothing. Of course, I'm not nothing. I am nowhere in the sense that I'm not contained in the fabric of reality. You could say I am that fabric, or what can be called my mind is. We've been through that. Let's say the fabric is in my imagination."

"In your imagination, you say?" I showed him a rascal grin. "So, it's not real, then."

"It's real to you, since you are contained in the same fabric. And it's real to me, since I make it and there is nowhere it is not. This is as real as it ever gets."

I had no trouble understanding that. To all the characters within a dream, it is real. The only one for whom it is not, is the dreamer. Well, even to him it is real as long as it lasts. No mystery there.

But I was not finished dissecting who this dreamer might be, and where he would come from.

"Didn't you say earlier in our conversation that you make the world and the world makes you? One cannot be without the other."

"Right. But remember – it's always. No starting point. No end. It is eternal interaction. Since I am nowhere, if there were not a world I would be nothing. And we both agree that's impossible. To paraphrase Descartes: I am, therefore the world is. The world is, therefore I am."

"You are the dreamer."

"You are my dream."

I raised my glass.

"Cheers to that!"

We let our glasses cling together and emptied them. I was quick to grab the bottle and refill them.

Before putting the bottle down again, I checked how much was left of the wine. The bottle was still almost full. Of course, I thought. I didn't mind at all.

"The difference between me and a dreamer," Cael resumed, "is that I make my dream. I shape it and govern it."

"Consciously, like someone being awake?"

"You can say I am consciousness, and the world is of what I am conscious. I prefer to call it awareness, though. I am aware of the world. Without the world, nothing could make me aware."

"And we can't have any nothing. But how can you be aware of yourself?"

"I am aware of what I make."

"Does that mean you don't really know who or what you are?"

"I'm nothing but what I make."

I leaned back to look at him from a little distance. Then I let out a grunt.

"You know what?" I said. "That sounds kind of sad."

Cael's xylophone started playing. It took a while to die out.

"I knew this meeting was a good idea," he said.

My Turn

Cael let his hand fall flat on the table. It made the glasses and the bottle bounce a little, but far from the point of tipping over.

"How about some dessert?"

I looked at the Latour bottle turned cornucopia.

"I haven't had enough of this marvelous wine yet," I said. "So, why don't we try some cheese with it?"

"That's a great idea," Cael replied and stood up.

The cheese table was just as lavish as the other stations of the buffet, with a lot of domestic as well as foreign varieties, covering the scale from pale and mild to blue and pungent. They were cut into cubes, which was convenient but not very visually appetizing. The piles of cubes made it all look industrial.

I picked a handful of samples, but not with my usual care. Too much of what had happened and what had been said continued to distract my mind. I mainly went by color, creating as wide a palette as possible from the assortment. Not the smartest thing to do. Anyway, I was sure the wine would have the power to forgive it all.

I didn't bother about bread, fruit or any other addition. I rarely do. Either the cheese speaks for itself, or it's not that much of a cheese. The good ones demand solitude on the plate. Solitude and veneration, like in a monastery.

As usual, Cael was less restrained. Before we returned to our table, he had a pile on his plate not looking much different from those at the cheese station. His body must indeed be an illusion of some kind, or it could not remain that slim with such eating habits. He sent me an amused glance.

As soon as we were seated at our table, I opened my mouth. So did he, but to stick in a cheese cube.

"I have one major problem with your cosmology," I said.

"Do you, now?" he responded, chewing on the cheese.

"It's that now thing. No real past, no future, as if they were only invented in the now."

"Not invented, but constantly revised. The past can't be revisited and the future not visited. There is only now."

"I can see how that may be true in a philosophical sense, or psychological for that matter. We perceive ourselves always in a now. But there is ample proof of a real past, leading to our now and extending beyond it as time goes on."

"Such as?"

"Evolution. Life on earth evolved from self-replicating molecules to one-cell organisms and on to the many species of today. There are plenty of fossils showing this progression. That demands a timeline. So does the development of every human being from the joining of a spermatozoon and an ovum, growing into a fetus, giving birth to a child, who grows to an adult, and eventually dies. A very real timeline for every one of us."

I paused shortly, but not long enough for Cael to respond. He did not seem to try, anyway, but kept himself busy with the cheese. He must have found it more of a treat than I did.

"Even the solar system shows many signs of a different past, as well as indications of its future. Most of them, like the orbits of the planets, are predictable. And look at the craters of the moon. They show past events, marking its surface for the future. The whole universe is full of traceable events. It's even made up by events. Something leads to something, which leads to something. The chain of events over time. Everything is on a course from the distant past to the distant future."

I was about to let Cael respond, when it hit me so suddenly that I blurted it out:

"Hell, you can even say that there is no now! There's just a timeline from the past to the future. The now is a fleeing moment, veritably non-existent. An infinitesimally small point in time, immediately passed. It doesn't exist. Time doesn't ever halt."

"Have a look at the clock," Cael suggested.

I didn't bother to do so. It would surely still show exactly the same time as last I checked. Or not. It didn't matter.

"Clocks can halt," I said. "But time goes on, as our conversation has done. Without time, how could we at all form a speech with word following word? No, I'd say time might be the only thing that exists. Or to be more precise, the chain of events from what has happened to what will happen. It's the now that is the illusion."

"That's one way of looking at it."

I frowned.

"Sure. But I prefer to use Ockham's razor, the simplest explanation. What could be simpler than a timeline, proven by everything around us, as well as by our own lifespan?"

"Numquam ponenda est pluralitas sine necessitate," Cael replied in what to my ears sounded like perfect Latin. "That's what Ockham's text states. Plurality is never to be posited without necessity. So, simplicity lies in the quantity. There's no multitude of events in complicated interaction making the world. It's all in the mind."

"There are many minds."

"No. Just one. A state of mind. In the now."

"Then how can you and I disagree?"

Cael tilted his head to the side and looked at me with what appeared to be both empathy and mockery.

"Don't you ever disagree with yourself?"

"Oh, constantly," I confessed with an exaggerated sigh. "But it just proves that even in my mind there is an ongoing process."

"All your thoughts are already there. You just bounce between them."

I inhaled to protest rather strongly, but Cael was quicker.

"We're talking past each other. Let me try again, with a different imagery."

I nodded and waited for him to continue. In the moment of silence, I picked one of the cheese cubes from my plate, the palest one in the set, and put it in my mouth. It was rather bland. The wine would wash it away already by its bouquet. I tried it and found that I was right.

Cael observed me while I conducted this little experiment. Then he spoke.

"The world is not one of things, but of thought. All thought. Let's call it the aether of the mind. It imagines the world of things and that makes them real – in the mind. They have no place outside of it. To the mind, they are still real. But only there. If the mind could forget, they would be gone. They depend on the mind being aware of them. That's why there is only a now. If the world doesn't exist in the now, it can be nowhere else. It can't be in the past. That would demand a now in which to observe it as a past, and a future it heads for. It can't be in the future, since that is by definition a consequence of the past and not yet in existence. There can only be now."

"In a manner of speaking," I muttered.

"The name that can be named is not the eternal name. Words can only do so much."

"The mind you speak of is yours, I presume."

"Yours, too. You exist only in your mind. Remember your childhood dream, where you are in the middle of your own head. The world you perceive, including your own body, is of your mind's making. It changes if you think of it differently, as it does in what you call your dreams. They are just as real, since they are figments of your imagination, like everything else. So is the timeline you speak of with such passion."

"But other minds see the same world. How would they do that if it's made by my imagination?"

"Do you know the difference between you and the others? Can you say for sure where your mind ends and those of others begin? It's one aether of the mind. You share a lot in it. More than you do not. Much more."

"Almost all of us agree that the world exists outside of our minds. That's what our minds tell us."

"It's what you tell your minds. You uphold that way of looking at it."

"It fits with our experience of it."

"Of course it does, since you decide what to experience. Of course your model of the world makes sense to you. How else could you agree on it? Mankind makes its world and holds on to it."

"Didn't you say that you make the world?"

"I make *the* world," Cael replied. "You make your world. You dream, but I dream the dream in which you all dream. I'm the mind from which all minds emerge. I am mind. I am thought. Your thoughts are echoes in my head."

"Oh, that must be quite some noise!"

Cael was amused, but not enough to play his xylophone.

"I have a big head. And there are many thoughts, but not as many as you might think. I told you that you humans share a lot. Your minds are alike. So are your thoughts. Some stick out, but most of them are just the same old same old. I hear them, but I don't listen."

"I'd do the same. As the years go by – imaginary or not – I find that more and more, I've heard it all before." I signed it with a sigh.

"All those fragments of mind that call themselves human, they dream up their own world and thereby also play with the fabric of reality. It's a flexible fabric. It has no laws, not even Tao. Anything that the mind can imagine is there. That's why I say it's all in the mind. There is nothing else, but that is everything."

"But how can anything ever change if it's all in the now?"

"I've told you. Everything is already there. You just hop between alternatives, reshaping the now. Your mind makes it real."

"Also the alternative of a timeline?"

"Also that. You're really fond of that idea, aren't you?"

"It's convenient."

I had another piece of cheese, this time a slightly more colorful one. That could also be said for its taste. Still, the wine was unchallenged. Cael popped several pieces into his mouth in quick succession and chewed ever so happily. Eating seemed to be a game to him.

As I was about to pick up another piece of cheese, a thought appeared in my mind, halting my hand.

"But wait a minute – if you pardon the expression," I said, flashing a grin. "If what we humans imagine to be real is real because of it, timeline and all – then it's no different from if that reality is real without our imagining it. Right?"

Now, I got to hear that charming xylophone playing again.

"That would be true, except for one thing."

"Pray tell."

"You don't really believe it."

"I don't?"

"You don't. And rightly so. Just like you can sometimes feel in the middle of a dream that it's a dream, you get glimpses of a reality beyond the one you imagine. You feel the dissonance."

*

Although it frustrated me, I had to admit to myself that Cael was not completely wrong. I could feel the dissonance. Otherwise I would not ponder so much the secrets of the universe I was sure were there to reveal. I would just settle for what science and human conventions preached, and go on with my life.

Since childhood, I had felt that those universal secrets were within reach. I had not gotten hold of them, but I was certainly still reaching.

To Cael, I had argued for Darwin's theory of evolution. And indeed, there is no way of denying it. A brilliant theory, applicable to so much more than biology. But I've always felt that it is not yet complete. Something is missing in it, something fundamental. As it stands, it leaves too much to chance. So, I've speculated that maybe animals have some kind of will-power able to influence mutations in the desired direction.

"That's it," Cael interrupted my thoughts. "The mind decides. There are no coincidences."

I didn't respond, since my thoughts were already moving along.

Also the idea of survival of the fittest, I've found a bit crude. This may be a man-eat-man world, but that's not all it is. There is beauty. There is longing and there are dreams.

Something else is going on, influencing both evolution and other chains of events.

The human brain is kind of an anomaly in evolution. As it started to grow, it was quickly detrimental to survival, long before it became the most powerful tool at our service. Children were born while still being mere fetuses, because their heads were getting as big as the female body was able to deliver. Outside the womb their survival was much more at risk than inside of it. And not only that. The growing brain was not economical. It demanded a lot of protein and other nutrition, again worsening man's chances of survival.

Still, the brain kept growing, until its proportion to the body was completely absurd in comparison to other animals. Why? Because we loved this emerging tool of ours. It opened the world to a brand new level of fascination. We wouldn't sacrifice it for anything, not even for a better chance of survival. Once we had tried it, we wanted nothing more than the increase of it. Our big brain was a wonderful toy for the mind.

I halted my line of thought, to check if Cael would butt in. He must have liked where I was going. But he just nodded minutely and smiled at me. So, I was the one feeling the need to comment.

"You like that, don't you?"

He shrugged his shoulders, but his smile turned into a grin.

Then my thoughts moved on to the Big Bang theory. I've always liked its simplicity and intriguing indications, but that doesn't mean I've subscribed to it completely. As I told Cael earlier in our conversation, I enjoyed the perspective of the whole universe popping up very much like an idea does in one's mind. It comes, seemingly out of nowhere, and it grows. As if by magic. Somehow, that rings so true to me.

But there is no way I would accept that this Big Bang came out of nothing. That would be impossible – and a big stain on an otherwise elegant theory. An ever pulsating universe of big bangs and big crunches would make more sense. So would, to a lesser extent, an eternal multiverse giving birth to universes all over. Just as with the theory of evolution, I've always felt that something essential is missing in the Big Bang theory. The key, I bet, is in that very initial event, the beginning of the bang. What banged?

"It's the end of the reach of your timeline," Cael said calmly.

"If so, why not a similar end in the future? But astronomy today states that the likeliest is a very slow and darkening decay of the universe as entropy increases, into infinity."

"That's because you believe the future is yet unmade. Your model carries this uncertainty. That direction of your timeline fades out ahead, like you believe the universe will."

"That's the case also if our timeline model exists outside of our minds. Contrary to the past, we have no concrete evidence of what the distant future will be."

Cael did not bother to reply. His silence, and the smile on his face, spoke volumes.

"Anyway," I resumed, "the anomalies will lead to new paradigms, and the missing pieces of the puzzle will be found. In my timeline, we move from ignorance to knowledge. Granted, it may be a bumpy ride at times. But we're getting there." Now it was my turn to grin, as I added teasingly, "In the future."

"That's no big deal, since you've already got it. You just need to realize that."

"And what is that, precisely? Don't tell me. It's all in the mind."

"Where else?"

*

For a while, we occupied our mouths with the cheese cubes and the Latour, the latter of which made my frustration melt away. One or other cheese was also able to sooth me, though none could measure up to the splendid wine.

Cael dug in with much more appetite and delight. The pile of cheese on his plate was shrinking fast. How much had he eaten so far from the buffet? Probably enough to make its steep price almost reasonable.

By the way, with all the staff gone, who would charge us? Our bill must be something else, considering the wines and all. With an inward smile – and some trepidation – I thought to myself that I hoped Cael's magic would not suddenly come to an end, when it was time to pay.

He looked up at me.

"Don't worry," he said. "It won't. It can't."

I gladly wanted to believe that.

*

I was pushing around one of the cheese cubes on the plate with my fork, unsure if I wanted it in my mouth. I had a sip of the wine instead.

"Cael," I started, keeping my eyes on him. "All your talk about the mind has made me realize one thing."

"And what might that be?" he asked, showing no sign of being possible to surprise.

"I know how you did all those magic tricks of yours." I made a sweeping gesture around me.

"You do, do you?" Cael inquired, putting his fork to rest on the plate in front of him and reaching for his wine glass.

"Hypnosis."

I said it with emphasis, like a contestant at a quiz show would pronounce the answer to the grand prize question when sure of being correct.

Cael made no response at all, neither in words nor in his facial expression. He looked at me, holding his glass but not lifting it.

"Everything could be done by hypnosis," I continued with confidence, if not to say defiance. "Also my sudden change to my younger self. Stopping the clocks, emptying the restaurant and lobby, the Latour bottle that keeps refilling itself. Everything. Easily."

Still no reaction at all from Cael.

"Once you got me in a hypnotic trance, you could make anything seem to happen and I would be convinced it did for real." I chuckled. "Then it would really be only in my mind."

I leaned back and waited for his response with a triumphant grin on my face, which embarrassed me a little. But I couldn't make it go away. Well, I was quite proud of my conclusion.

Cael kept his face absolutely neutral, pinning my eyes with his. There was a long silence. I was getting uncomfortable, but also increasingly curious about what his response would be. So, I waited it out.

Finally he opened his mouth, slowly, and said with a clear voice:

"Yes."

*

The single word made me twitch, as if he had reached over and snapped the tip of my nose with his finger.

"Yes?" I checked, as if doubting my ears.

He nodded.

"What do you mean? Yes as in 'yes, you're hypnotized' or as in 'yes, it really is only in your mind'?"

"What's the difference?"

"Well, for one thing, when I get out of a hypnotic trance, everything is back to normal."

"How would you know?"

I opened my mouth to reply, but halted. It hit me that I needed to think about it.

"Remember Chuang Tzu's dream about the butterfly," Cael added.

That was exactly what I had done, together with other bits and pieces of our conversation. It is not that easy to ascertain what is real and what is not. But I was not going to give him that.

"I told you before, I will know when the world is outside me, and not only in my head. When I wake up from a dream, I know it was a dream. I only need to snap out of the hypnotic trance to know I was in one."

Cael released his wine glass and put his hand on mine, resting on the table. Again I had that sweet tickling sensation all through my body. It made me think I had wasted a lot of our time together playing with words, instead of just enjoying the moment and the company of this handsome young man, who had been so kind – for whatever reason – to spend his time with me.

He leaned even closer, until his face almost filled my view. I got lost in his dark eyes.

"Good luck with that," he said without any irony, but with so much benevolence, it felt like he was a priest giving me his blessing.

For some reason, my eyes moistened. Maybe I sighed. I did exhale until my lungs were all but empty.

Cael leaned back, grabbing his glass again and lifting it to take a sip. As he did so, I became aware of the surroundings. The Peacock Alley restaurant was full of guests, their utensils clinging as they dug into the many temptations from the buffet. Waiters circulated the many tables. Cooks were working at the buffet tables. The pianist was back by the grand piano, singing and playing some pop song I didn't recognize. At the lobby, clerks were busy with the flow of hotel guests checking in and out.

I looked at that dreadful clock towering over the buffet. It was half past two. A quick check confirmed that so was the clock on my cell phone. Our table was back at its original size and the black marble pillar had returned to one side of it. The Latour bottle was almost empty.

My eyes found their way back to Cael, who was sipping wine and looking around, not at me. I waited until he did.

I was overcome by sadness. I had no idea why. He looked at me with an expression that could be inquisitive, as if he was a bit surprised to see me there. Or it could be that he expected me to say something. I didn't know what. I just gaped.

I must have looked rather silly, but Cael was nowhere near to play a xylophone solo.

"I've had a great time," he said with a wonderfully humming voice. "I hope you have, too."

I nodded repeatedly, still unable to speak.

"We must do this again, some time," he continued and stood up.

He extended his hand. I shook it, not even thinking of standing up.

"Don't worry about the bill," he assured me. "I'll take care of it."

And he left.

*

I watched Cael's back until it disappeared in the direction of the hotel foyer. Somehow, it felt wrong.

I had not expected him to be the first one to leave. I was usually the one leaving first. I was usually the one getting bored with whatever company. But I quickly had to confess to myself that if he didn't leave, I never would. Never. And I didn't even get to know his surname.

The waiter came to clear the table of Cael's plate and utensils. There was still a little wine in the bottle. I emptied it into my glass and handed him the bottle.

A creeping sense of worry made me ask him if the bill had been settled.

"By the young gentleman, yes," the waiter assured me. "Quite handsomely, at that," he added with an appreciative smile and a little nod.

I remained in my chair, sipping slowly of the wine in my glass. It was still impressive, but some of its pleasing power had evaporated.

I didn't touch the cheese on my plate, nor was I the least tempted to explore the mountains of desserts and cakes the brunch buffet had to offer. When I had finished the wine in my glass, I stood up. It was almost three o'clock. I felt rather heavy, but I trusted that the walk back to my hotel would give me back some of my vigor.

As I passed the grand piano on the way out, the pianist started playing *The Final Countdown*, a rather dramatic worldwide hit from the 1980's by the Swedish rock group Europe.

I found myself walking to the beat of the music. It was embarrassing, but I was quickly out of the pianist's reach, entering the foyer and then in no time out the Waldorf Astoria doors.

Asked for It

As I stepped out on Park Avenue, a wind sweeping down the wide avenue made my jacket dance and whisked around my hair. I took a deep breath and felt my gloom losing its grip on me. The wind blew it away.

Cars hurried by on the street, most of them yellow cabs. The many pedestrians on the sidewalk showed the same hurry, this way or that. I refused to follow their tempo, so I frequently got in their way. I could hear some grunts, and one or two bumped into me with a force that could very well be intentional. But I didn't care.

The trees along the avenue were lush with green leaves. The tall buildings hid most of the sky, but what I could see of it was light blue with just spots of friendly white clouds. I took another deep breath and decided to make my promenade to the hotel a detour. Why not just walk without a goal, and see where I would end up?

It was not like I was hungry. I could spend a few hours on the streets of Manhattan. That was what I had come here for. Maybe later an espresso at some coffee shop, preferably not Starbucks or any of the other chains.

I lit a cigarette. When I inhaled the smoke eagerly, I realized that I had not had one in hours. Odd. I was usually – well, always – reminded of my habit in much less time. Anyway, smoking this one was even more enjoyable when it was so long since the last one.

I was not the only one smoking on the sidewalk, but we were so few I took the precaution of avoiding blowing smoke in the face of any other pedestrian. It reminded me of sneaking away into hiding to get a smoke when I was a high school kid, so long ago. It was a complicated, but it also added kind of a spice to the smoke I inhaled with such eagerness.

Same here on Park Avenue. The thrill of being kind of naughty. The slightly pink smoke was turning red from the glow of the cigarette, revealing how deep and hasty my puffs on it were.

The light of the crosswalk I just reached turned to WALK, so I decided to change my course and go to the other side of the street, although it was in the shadow. Halfway across, I changed my mind as I glanced back at the sunny side of the street.

But when I got back on that sidewalk, a cloud moved in to cover the sun. Now, both sidewalks were in the shade. So typical.

I knew what was going to happen. Sure enough. When the cloud had moved on to let the sunlight through again, it shone on the other sidewalk. But I was not going to let that get to me. I continued my walk on the shaded side of the street. It was not cold, so I was fine.

It was a pity with the trees, though. After a few minutes, the shade made the trees shed their leaves for the night, although it was just late afternoon. Soon, all the branches were barren and all of us pedestrians were kicking around the leaves at our feet. They painted the pavement green. Then they reddened, as they started to wither.

The wind got hold of lots of them, filling the air with red leaves fluttering like butterflies.

I had to blink when occasional leaves hit my face. But they were already turning brown and starting to pulverize. The wind would clean the air as well as the street in no time.

Passing a small coffee shop, I stopped to peek through the window. Its interior looked so charming and peaceful, with a few scattered customers. I was tempted to get in. But a coffee now would just spoil my appetite. Instead, I walked on and lit another cigarette. It tasted even better than the previous one.

I knew that I would soon spend a couple of hours in a restaurant, where no smoking was allowed, so I might as well smoke a few while I had the chance.

Both the air and the pavement were already cleared of leaves. With this wind it was what to expect. On the other side of Park Avenue, the sun was still shining. So, the trees there were full of green leaves. Should I get over there, after all?

But then I would have to cross the wide street, with all the quickly moving cars, buses, tanks, trucks, and bikes. Not the safest thing. Although it was Sunday, the traffic was too intense.

There was no gap in sight between the vehicles, and on this straight and wide street they were rushing with a speed at least the 55 miles per hour permitted. Some of the motorcycles zigzagging between the cars were probably doing 70 or even 80. So, I stayed on my sidewalk.

But it was getting increasingly crowded. I decided to walk closer to the buildings, so I could keep my slow pace without irritating too many other pedestrians.

It was a good thing I did, because soon I saw a parade approaching from ahead, filling the whole sidewalk.

It was headed by acrobatic clowns hopping and doing somersaults, so it had to be a circus. Right behind them was a brass band playing so loud that as they got nearer, even the cars on the street were inaudible. Between the musicians, I spotted glimpses of horses and tigers, and at the far end of the parade were a couple of elephants swinging their trunks. Did they do it to the beat of the music? Hard to tell.

I stepped aside, leaning my back against the wall of a building, waiting for the parade to pass. Only the tigers bothered to glance at me. They must have been recently fed, since they showed no interest in me after a quick glance. It didn't even seem like they got my scent.

I had to duck not to get hit by the swinging trunk of one of the elephants. But it was looking straight ahead, so that was surely accidental. Soon the parade has passed and I could continue my promenade.

After just a little while I felt that my feet were sore. It was starting to get quite painful. I glanced at them, and to my surprise they were on the pavement. I was walking on my feet. Why would I do that? No wonder they were sore.

I looked around. Several of the passers-by were staring at me. I hurried to get my hands on the ground and lift my legs in the air, starting to walk on my hands like everybody else. In seconds, the pain in my feet subsided. People stopped staring and went on with their business.

Still, I was glad to escape the crowd when I entered the foyer of the Waldorf Astoria.

Since I was indoors and the floor was covered by a carpet, I decided to get down from my handstand and walk on my feet again. I saw that most of the guests did the same.

I continued to the lobby area, where the Peacock Alley restaurant was serving its famous Sunday brunch. I checked the hideous clock towering in the middle of all the buffet tables loaded with food. It was eleven sharp. I was just in time for my reservation. And the walk had made me hungry.

I told the hostess my name and she led me directly to a table for two, right by the side of one of the many black marble pillars. She pulled out the chair for me, but I stopped momentarily.

There was a young man sitting on the opposite chair. I had a quick look around. There were several empty tables in sight. Why would she pair me up with someone else? Was the restaurant really fully booked?

He looked up at me with a very friendly smile. I would be extremely impolite to protest the seating.

"Welcome back, Stefan," he said with a mellow voice. "I hope you had a nice walk."

I landed on my chair and the hostess disappeared. At that instant, I remembered everything.

"So, have you snapped out of the hypnotic trance?"

"Evidently not," I mumbled.

Then I heard that melodic xylophone laugh again.

"Trust me," Cael said when he had finished laughing, which took a little while. "There is nothing to snap out of."

*

Cael was cheerful, flashing his white teeth again and again. He convinced me to try the desserts. I failed to muster any resistance.

"I'm sure you have some appetite after your promenade," he said. "But we can't take the brunch from the top again, can we?"

It was with the desserts that the Waldorf Astoria brunch menu really went bananas. In addition to the countless cakes and puddings and mousses and cookies and truffles, they had a grand chocolate fountain and a cook was blowtorching Alaska lollipops of ice cream covered with meringue. A calorie crescendo.

But I had lost my sweet tooth already when entering puberty, so I settled for berries covered with dark chocolate from the fountain and a slice of what looked like a Tarte Tatin, but with pear instead of apple.

Cael, on the other hand, filled his plate as unabashed as usual. How could he remain so slender? There was no sign of his belly protruding the least, in spite of all that he had eaten so far. Another time trick? The clock was slightly past eleven. Maybe what he ate before the clock returned had disappeared with the time when he ate it.

Not so with me. I was still full. It was strange. Before reentering the hotel, mere minutes ago, I had not been. On my promenade, I had actually felt some appetite building. Maybe the mountains of sweets filled me up through my eyes. I found the sight close to disgusting. Too much, just too much.

When we returned to our table, a bottle of Chateau d'Yquem was standing in the middle of it, and two appropriate glasses were placed by our seats.

Why was I not surprised? The most exclusive of dessert wines, its golden liquid carrying the heavenliest sweetness to be found. I have no sweet tooth, but this wine was irresistible. I had tried it before, merely once or twice, and was nothing but delighted at doing it again.

Anyway, there was simply no way we would be able to empty the bottle. There is too much even of a good thing. In this case a very good thing, but still.

Well, that would take care of itself, when the moment arrived. As soon as we were seated, Cael poured the luscious liquid into our glasses and we even forgot to toast before drinking. There was no disappointment. I let the rich golden aftertaste fondle my tongue and took deep breaths to indulge in it.

There was really no pastry needed with it.

"I sure hope that you'll pay for this too, Cael."

"Don't worry. I made it for us."

I frowned, but with my lips forming a little smile. I had no reason to complain. I took another sip, not even thinking of trying the desserts yet. Cael, though, hurried to dig in. He had a lot on his plate to go through.

I observed him for a while. He didn't give any sign of noticing, as if engulfed by the sweets before him.

"You've really been playing me like a fiddle from the moment we met, haven't you?"

Now, he looked up, still chewing on a piece of cake. He had an expression of innocence. But as I scrutinized it, I found it to be closer to a tease. Were it not for his good looks, I would get grumpy. As it was, I just couldn't. Aren't we all suckers for beauty?

"If so," he said as his smile got more prominent in his expression, "I do it all the time."

"Why me?"

He shook his head slightly, almost invisibly.

"I do it with everyone and everything. I'm the world maker, you know."

"So you've told me. And you've made a lot, no doubt. As for the world, though, I still have my doubts. But that's not what I mean."

"Do you still believe you're hypnotized?"

"That's as good an explanation as any. Actually better than most."

"Alright, then. Close enough." He let out a few tones of his laughter.

"But why me? Why would a world maker spend so much time on me, inquiring with such curiosity about my life and my misconceptions, supposedly, of cosmology?"

"You asked for it."

"I did?" I said, full of doubt. "How?"

"Let me remind you of something you have said here at the brunch." Then he switched to a voice which sounded exactly like mine does in my own ears. Exactly. "'Ever since childhood, I've felt that I am on an exploration. Some would call it a quest, but it feels much more like research. Gathering information, analyzing and coming to conclusions. I've done it through my writing, my painting, my aikido practice. Well, my whole life. Everything I've been up to is part of my exploration. And what I've tried to explore is the true nature of the universe, what this whole thing is all about. I have to confess that I settle for nothing less.'"

It was weird to have him quote me with my own voice, as if playing a recording. Spooky.

"But I said that when we had already met and spent some time here."

Cael shook his head in an almost patronizing way, but his closed lips formed a smile that softened it considerably.

"There you go with that time thing again," he scolded me. "Are you trying to pretend that you said it only on the spur of the moment? You claimed it was true for your whole life."

"So, you've heard me before."

"I know you."

"And you're here to enlighten me?"

He was amused, but just enough for a chuckle. No xylophone.

"I'm no preacher. Anything you are able to understand, you already know. You just have to put the pieces together. I believe you said something earlier, which suggested you know that, too. It's all up to you. This is just a conversation."

"Well, from my side it has mostly been a kind of confession, really. As for what you have said, it has come quite close to a lecture."

"That's how you want it."

I confirmed it with my silence. And I had another sip of the Yquem, which was still lovely. The desserts on my plate remained untouched.

"What you do with it," Cael continued, "that's for you to decide. I'm enjoying myself, nonetheless."

So was I, of course. It had been upsetting at times, every so often confusing, even frustrating. But I had enjoyed it, and wouldn't want to be without it. Food for thought, surpassing that of the buffet.

That was probably what drove me back to the Peacock Alley restaurant after my promenade – hypnosis or no hypnosis.

"We should do this again," I said half jokingly.

"It will be exactly the same."

"I mean we should do it after some time, when I..." I stopped myself, remembering Cael's attitude towards the concept of a timeline. "Forget it."

He was kind enough to hold back his laughter. Nor did he comment on forgetting, although I was sure he would regard that as impossible – at least for him.

"You've played games with my mind, Cael. That's for sure. But I admit my mind is good at that all by itself. And there's really no way for me to notice when it does. In that way it is, as you keep saying, real. What I ask myself is not if it's real, but if it's the only thing that's real. Isn't everything real?"

"That's what I say."

"Then I can choose whatever reality tickles my fancy, and it won't make any difference. I can pursue the idea of a universe existing outside my mind, or one only existing in my mind. It will be the same."

"Mostly, yes."

"In what way will it not be the same?"

"You won't like this," he said, "but it won't be as real. At some point, only one model will stand the test of scrutiny."

"At what point?"

"Several, actually. The first one you already experience. Only one of the models agrees with your intuition.

You have confessed to that. What you claim to know is not what your intuition tells you. Regarding what you have found out about the universe, you said, 'It's not at all what it seems to be.'"

This time, he did not bother to change his voice into mine when he quoted me, for which I was thankful.

"But there is more," Cael continued. "The cosmological theories you cherish will not mend all anomalies. The math will falter. Experience will reveal the absurdities. Not in everyday life, but at extremities."

"Like the celestial mechanics of Newton did fine, until we had instruments exact enough to confirm Einstein?" I suggested.

"Like psychology gets stuck when presupposing that the mind is a tool for the body, instead of the other way around. The mind will remain a mystery, until this is corrected. I don't mean behavior, but the mind itself. Thought. Fantasy. Dreams."

"A lot of what the brain does and how it does it can be explained by evolutionary biology."

"A lot, certainly. How else could you persist with that idea? But a lot is not all. I'm not talking about what fits with what you admit to knowing, but with all that you really know. What you hide from yourself. I enjoy speaking with you because I see you are struggling with that illusion, a struggle that eventually smashes it. You are near."

"I must confess that I feel that, too. But it might just be my hubris."

"Then hooray for hubris! Get up from the chair!"

*

We were talking faster and with more emphasis than before, as if hurrying towards some finishing line. We were quite loud, as well, but nobody around us seemed to mind. They showed no sign of being aware of our presence.

My heart was beating faster. I was searching for the question or comment that would solve the discrepancy between Cael's world view and mine. I had the nagging sensation that it was right on the tip of my tongue. It was so frustrating, I could have bitten my tongue if that would let it out.

Somehow, the cosmos Cael and I described was the same. Or there was a way of looking at the world, which explained both of them. I was sure of it. It was so near. My brain was boiling. But how to find it?

"Just say what comes to your mind," Cael urged me. "Right now."

I stared at him, without really looking. My head was spinning, faster and faster. My eyes were suddenly unable to focus, so everything was a blur.

Was I about to faint? I had stopped breathing. My whole chest cramped. It hurt. My body screamed inaudibly for fresh air. The lungs ached to empty themselves of air, in order to inhale again. I struggled with it, unable to find the command in my brain that would override the cramp in my chest. My heart raced. Would it pop? Could I take this?

Long seconds passed. I urged my brain to come up with something, anything, to get me out of this limbo. But it was blank. As if the brain had evaporated, leaving the skull hollow. My despair kept searching for any remaining brain cell to save me. I found none. The emptiness was a vacuum, tearing me apart from inside out.

A strange buzz in that void increased, and I remembered that exact feeling from childhood. It used to come when I was about to pass out, which happened frequently back then.

The void, the buzz, the lack of breath, the panic. That

was what always happened right before I fainted. The tilt of a pinball machine. A computer system shutdown. Like dying.

The buzz would intensify, as would my dizzy spell, in a spiral hurried on by itself. Then I'd black out and fall to the floor.

I hated it. The vulnerability, the nausea, the embarrassment of waking up to find myself surrounded by curious classmates in the classroom. It often happened there, and I got to understand that it was because I was not allowed to leave my chair when it started.

If I had just laid down on the floor when the first signs of it came, it might have passed instead of increased. But I could not. I was stuck in that chair, so I couldn't avoid it. Once it started, that inner buzz, I was helpless to change its course.

My frantic resistance actually made those attacks worse. Somehow, I refused to faint. I refused to lose consciousness. That buzz got louder, the void grew bigger and the dizziness increased, without the release of passing out. I extended and worsened the anguish of the nausea in an effort to avoid fainting.

It worked. A child making up his mind is a powerful thing. But it was not for the better.

Those prolonged torments took their toll. When they finally subsided, I was sweaty and pale as a corpse, fatigued for hours, like an amateur marathon runner after the race. An ordeal, draining me completely.

Not only were the attacks dreadful while they lasted, which was longer and longer each time. But I feared them so much, I had a tendency to induce them when I was tense enough to worry they would come. They came because I worried too much that they would. A vicious circle, hard to keep from spinning faster.

Oddly, although I usually had those attacks in the classroom because I couldn't escape, my teacher didn't notice, once I stopped fainting. I was sure of twisting in agony. But she never saw it. She thought I was making it up, for some reason. Why would I ever do that?

I believed it was something I just had to live with, an irreparable malfunction of mine. There was no broken leg, no nosebleed, just something my mind did to me. So, I thought there was nothing to do about it.

But when I was thirteen, I finally managed to talk to the school nurse about it. She said something about nerves and gave me Valium pills. They made no difference.

My mother took me to the hospital, where they checked me with EEG. They were ruling out epilepsy. Then they sent me to a psychologist.

After a few sessions, he explained to me that it was my imagination running wild, causing the attacks. He had no solution and nothing more to tell me, so he stopped the sessions. Well, he prescribed more and stronger Valium.

I thought Valium was just sugar pills, *placebo*, because it had no effect at all on me. Instead, I learned to distract myself when I felt an attack on the way. At the very first sign of it, I interrupted the vicious circle by thinking of something else. By time, I got better at it. Having a cigarette, leaving the room if I could, but mainly trying my best to think about something else.

When I reached my twenties, the attacks had become so rare I was starting to think they were permanently gone. They were not. But there were years between them, then decades.

I must have been in my thirties when I realized that they were caused by panic disorder. It was something unknown to that psychologist I met as a child in the 1960's. Hopefully, children of today can be spared from it by some therapeutic method or pharmaceuticals that don't make them lethargic.

Me, I had finally learned to manage quite well on my own. Also, as an adult, I found that I could almost always leave. Even before the buzz, I would get out into the open air and take a few deep breaths. That would solve it. Mostly. So, I rarely had to. The thought alone could usually stop that vicious circle.

But here I was with a body in cramp and lungs refusing to work. The buzz, the vertigo, the nausea – they all increased. I was stuck within that dreadful circle. I felt like I was about to die. It was almost so that I looked forward to it. Anything to get out of this excruciation!

Then it suddenly appeared to me, as a sentiment more than a word: Accept! Don't fight it. Go with it.

Why had I not thought of it before? Because that child in my past overruled it once. He did not want to faint anymore, so he resisted, resisted, resisted. Regardless of the toll it took. And he had kept his grip on me ever since. There was no way I could unlock. I didn't have the key.

That little boy held on to it, back in the time of his decision. The key was still there, in the long ago, and nowhere else.

But it was that child calling out to me now, from long ago and deep inside the void. Accept! He allowed it. He urged me.

With an overwhelming rush of gratitude, I did. I fainted.

Out of the Chair

When I opened my eyes, I found myself lying on a carpeted floor. It was quite soft, so I was comfortable. Slowly, I became aware of the room I was in, from my spot on the carpet and out, then up. It was big, with a lot of furniture.

The noise around me also increased, as I tried to figure out where I was and how I had gotten there.

A young man in a black suit and white shirt was kneeling beside me. When he gently placed his hand on my shoulder I looked up at his face.

It was pale, although his hair was pitch-black. So were his eyebrows. His lips were sculpted to have a seductive smile built in to them, as if very keen on kissing. I wouldn't mind.

He was handsome, indeed. When I noticed the sort of Japanese shape of his eyes I also recognized him. It was Ezra Miller, the movie actor. What was he doing here? He smiled at me, showing glimpses of his shiny white teeth. Nice guy.

I looked around again. Now, the place was familiar to me. The Peacock Alley restaurant of the Waldorf Astoria. Sunday brunch. I remembered.

Looking back at the young man's face, still smiling ever so sweetly, I knew it was Cael. He nodded, hearing my thoughts as usual.

"I got out of the chair," I said. My voice was low and weak, but I managed to make my words clear.

"You sure did," Cael replied. "Good for you."

When I started to move, he helped me up from the

floor. I was a bit unsteady at first, but soon I could stand on my own two feet without support.

I saw our table right next to where we were standing, but I was in no hurry to sit down. I took a deep breath, exhaling audibly through my mouth.

I felt unusually relaxed and sort of cleansed, like after a long time in the shower. I could move as I pleased, easily, but I had no urge to do so. I preferred to remain on the spot, savoring the moment. Cael patiently remained beside me.

We stood there, very still, for quite a while. I loved it. Although it was in the middle of the Waldorf Astoria, it felt like we were on the top of a countryside hill, with a fresh breeze in our faces and the many scents of nature in our nostrils. There may have been tears in my eyes.

The minutes felt like hours. No clock would justly measure the time that passed. Finally, I opened my mouth:

"I found something out, when I had that attack. Or maybe it was when I was passed out."

"Pray tell."

I looked at his hand on my shoulder, hoping he would never remove it, and then right into his dark Japanese eyes.

"I am you."

*

Cael leaned so close to my face, our noses were about to touch. His eyes were black holes. I could feel myself losing to their gravitational pull.

"Everyone is," he said.

Then my ears picked up the pianist as he started a new song. It was Eric Burdon's *All Is One* from the 1960's. A strange choice for a bar pianist. He sang the opening lines, with a voice lacking so much compared to that of Burdon:

We are one
I'm a part of you
You are part of me
We're all one.

Cael leaned back and winked at me.

"You're funny," I said to him.

"Aren't we all?"

I nodded a few times in agreement.

"When it comes to bringing meaning to life," I said with a voice that was still rather weak, "humor is right up there with art. If nothing else, we can laugh at it all. Well, sometimes we can. Usually."

I glanced at our table with the dessert dishes and the Chateau d'Yquem. I was not tempted. Nor was I inclined to sit down on my chair. Standing up made breathing easier.

Cael's hand on my shoulder kept me relaxed.

"I guess we're finished with the brunch," I mumbled. "I've had all I can take."

"I guess we are," Cael replied with that mellow voice close to a cat's purr.

In a glimpse, it struck me that he could be one. His slender elegance, his smooth movements, his penetrating eyes, his soothing purr. Just like a cat. I blinked repeatedly to get the idea out of my head, worrying that he would change into one. I preferred him as an Ezra Miller lookalike.

I glanced at him and found to my relief that he was still the same. A quick grin practically made his face split in two.

"As you wish," he said. Unfortunately he also removed his hand from my shoulder, albeit slowly and with a very elegant movement. "We say good bye for now."

"Isn't that always, in your book?"

"Or never."

We both laughed a little, more out of friendliness than any particular amusement. To me, this was in itself a sign that we had explored every subject and angle, some more than once. There was not really anything else to say, at least not at this point.

I might get a *dans l'escalier,* in the staircase, as the French put it. An idea appearing at the moment we parted. Probably. But so be it.

"Are you still inclined to believe you're hypnotized?" Cael wondered.

I shrugged my shoulders, feeling a bit guilty about it.

"It makes no difference," he assured me.

Then he extended his hand and I grabbed it, rather eagerly. I looked into those dark Japanese eyes and knew I would miss him as soon as I turned away.

"Good bye, Stefan," he said with no more of a smile than what came naturally for those lips of his. It was quite sufficient.

"Good bye, Cael."

We shook hands.

"You realize it's not my real name, don't you?"

"I suspected as much. If you have a name, it's probably just as elusive as your real form."

He nodded.

"Probably," he said and nodded a couple of times.

I was feeling all kinds of second-thoughts about putting an end to our conversation.

"Tell me, will we meet again?"

"Stefan, I'm forever right here," he replied and raised his free hand to put the tip of his index finger on my forehead. "You meet me whenever you like."

His words were deeply comforting, although I doubted it would be that easy. I wanted to hug him, but at the same time I felt it would be too awkward. After all, he might be no more than a figment of my imagination.

"Good bye," I said, not knowing what else to utter.

"Good bye."

I let go of his hand, which was not easy. Then I turned around and started walking towards the Waldorf Astoria foyer. But after just a couple of steps, seeing the exit to the foyer before me, I halted and turned back towards him.

"Is this when I die?"

It was an inkling that itched my mind already before I fainted. When I came to, the inkling had grown into a clear thought. I was not sure why. But it gnawed.

Well, if Cael would really be the world maker, it made sense that I didn't have much more to expect of life after meeting him. Even if he was not, this Sunday brunch had been strange enough to serve as an end scene. What more would there be to do? Where could I possibly go from here? So, I was more than a little bit apprehensive.

Now, at the moment of parting from Cael, I had to ask. He stood still. I saw no particular expression in his face. When he spoke, his voice was as calm as ever.

"Don't worry about dying. Nothing happens."

"You know I don't believe in nothing."

His charming smile reappeared.

"So, you have nothing to worry about."

I sort of grunted, but so low that he probably did not hear it. Then I turned around and walked towards the foyer. Just as I was about to lose sight of our table at the Peacock Alley, I glanced over my shoulder. Cael was gone. I didn't expect anything else.

I strode across the pompous Waldorf Astoria foyer and was out the door within a minute. It was raining.

www.ingramcontent.com/pod-product-compliance
Lightning Source LLC
LaVergne TN
LVHW041709070526
838199LV00045B/1264